END STREET VOLUME 2

RJ SCOTT
AMBER KELL

Love Lane Books

End Street Volume 2

Including: **The Case of the Dragon's Dilemma & The Case of the Sinful Santa**

Copyright ©2013-2015, 2024 Amber Kell, Copyright ©2013-2015, 2024 RJ Scott

Cover design by Meredith Russell, Published by Love Lane Books Limited

ISBN: 9781785645655

For everyone who loves End Street, and always for our families.

THE CASE OF THE

Dragon's Dilemma

END STREET VOLUME 2

Chapter One

"AND YOU'RE SURE YOU ARE GOING TO BE OKAY LOOKING after our little guest?" Bob didn't look convinced even as he asked.

"I'll be absolutely fine," Mikhail said firmly. "It's not like she does or says anything. She just sits there." He crossed his arms over his chest and looked squarely at the small blonde-haired girl curled up on a temporary bed with her thumb in her mouth. He knew absolutely nothing about children, other than that they were shouting, squealing bundles of confusion that he couldn't quite get his head around. But at least this one was quiet. She hadn't said a single word since being rescued from the docks and the cage she had been held in. The fact that she had been one of the children in the cages was another contradiction. He could understand Mal being in a cage—the small vampire was a spitfire and constantly back-chatting and, by all accounts, had made life difficult for her captors. This child, though—why would any human think she was threat enough to cage her?

"We don't know what her species is," Bob reminded him. "I could stay here and back you up." There was no trace of sarcasm in Bob's voice, but there was an element of slyness there that Sam picked up instantly.

"You're not staying here," Sam said firmly. "We have two schools to check out with Mal and she needs both her guardians with her."

Bob muttered something under his breath but didn't argue his position with any conviction. "You know I would never let you go on your own," he said a little louder. "But couldn't we interview them by phone or something?"

Mikhail chuckled. Bob was handling having to find a school with Sam for their surrogate daughter, in about the same easy way as Mikhail was handling having children around him at all.

"I don't have anywhere to be," Mikhail confirmed. "I don't mind sitting and watching."

"See if you can get her to talk," Sam suggested. "We can't return her to her people if we don't even know what species she is."

Mal ran into the room and slid to a stop next to Sam. She grabbed at his jacket to stop from falling on the wooden floor.

"Sam," she said quickly. "It's time to go."

Mikhail waved them away and shut the front door after they left. He wandered through the house and spent a short while in the file room, but Teddy was lurking and the disapproving looks from the ghost had him leaving to go and check on the girl. For a while, he hovered at the door. Sam had tried talking to her. Bob had attempted cajoling her. Smudge had even spent an inordinate amount of time winding in and out of her legs every time she stood up.

Still nothing.

Maybe he should give it a try. He did have one advantage over Bob in that his friend was a pure vampire. And over Sam, who was a human. Maybe she would react differently if she knew more about Mikhail? That he wasn't pure vampire. Maybe she was a mixed species and had learned not to share that fact with others. A lot of paranormals shunned mixed race beings because they weren't all one or the other.

It was worth a try at least. What did he have to lose?

He dragged a chair from the side of the room, straddled it backward, resting his chin on his hands. Where to start?

"So, I'm Mikhail," he began. She stared right at him and even stopped twirling her hair to listen. "I found out that I wasn't who I thought I was. It was hard to come to terms with finding out my entire life had been a lie. People didn't accept me. Even friends I'd known for a long time became enemies." Great; if anything, the confused expression on the little girl's face showed exactly how little of what he was saying made sense. "Let me start again."

She shuffled a little on the bed but still said nothing.

"I was about your age…well, ten anyway—hell, if you are even ten, that is—when I found out my dad wasn't my dad. Turns out I wasn't the full-blooded siren, or prince, I was expected to be. In fact, I'm half vampire. Before I was ten, you couldn't have told I was different from other children my age." Mikhail shook his head. He recalled the teasing and bullying when he couldn't master breathing underwater for long periods of time without using magic, and how he'd learned to pretend everything was okay. Sirens could breathe underwater without magic, and that was the first sign he wasn't 100 percent siren. A fact the court sycophants ignored for fear of upsetting Mikhail's father. As the middle son to the siren king, Mikhail hadn't been allowed to fail, and no one was brave enough to point out to King Haniel that Mikhail was odd. Even though they never failed to point it out to Mikhail himself whenever the king wasn't around. Did this child in front of him have the same problems? Had she been bullied, or pushed to one side? Was she *different*?

Mikhail sighed. "As I grew up, my vampire nature became dominant, and my siren side became quieter and in the background. I know what it's like to not be the same as everyone else and to have to keep secrets."

Was that enough to communicate what he wanted? Would she see that he understood if she was a half-breed or unusual species type?

She uncurled and sat up.

"Eliza," she said softly. "My name is Eliza."

"Hey, Eliza," Mikhail said. He kept his voice low and friendly. "Can you tell me how to get hold of someone who might be missing you? Parents? Family?"

Becoming mute again, she shook her head and clambered down off the bed. She walked past Mikhail and into the hallway before going into the bathroom. Well, at least he'd gotten her name. That was a start. She shut the door behind her, and Mikhail contemplated what he was going to ask her next. Maybe a location, or a surname, or anything that meant she could get home.

The door flew open again and, startled, Mikhail turned to look. What he saw had him on his feet in an instant with fangs exposed and a knife in each hand.

A siren—a filthy siren, dripping water everywhere. He had a glass box in one hand and held Eliza with the other. Eliza squirmed to get free, but the siren appeared strong and determined. Mikhail assessed the situation in a second, taking in the surprise on the siren's face, which quickly changed into a sneer, and the fear on Eliza's. He leaped for the siren with knives extended. Silver and iron blades sliced through one forearm and across the siren's chest. The siren yelled in pain and stumbled back into the bathroom, sliding on puddles of water and only stopping when he collided with another siren. Mikhail straightened from his leap and quickly jumped into the confusion of the bathroom. The whirlpool and waterfall were agitated and spitting water everywhere.

Mikhail didn't stop to wonder how the hell two sirens had managed to enter Sam's house. Instead, he dived with his knives in a firm hold and attacked the siren holding Eliza. In seconds he had cut the unwanted visitor enough that the siren dropped Eliza and cowered in shock.

"Run!" Mikhail shouted, "Eliza, run!"

She crawled away from the fallen siren who overcame his fear of Mikhail enough to grab her ankle. She screamed. Then the noise changed. Instead of remaining a plea for safety, it grew and grew until Mikhail and both sirens had to put their hands over their ears. The noise was unearthly, a screeching, echoing song, then it changed and Mikhail could almost make out words. As soon as the screech ended, Mikhail reacted instantly. He spun on his feet and buried both knives to the hilt in the injured siren—one in the throat and one through the heart. Now he couldn't get back up and attack Eliza again.

The other siren stood between Eliza and the door—he'd evidently moved in anticipation of her running, and his expression was one of success. Mikhail struggled to pull his knives from the fallen attacker's body and finally freed one from the flesh and muscle it had torn.

"Mikhail!" Eliza screamed. She was in the corner under the ornate sink and curled into the smallest shape she could be. The siren had got hold of her arm, attempting to pull her out as she kicked and struggled. Mikhail swiped at the siren with his knife and missed as the siren ducked. Mikhail swept back for another try, but his foot slipped on water and the siren took the chance to grab his wrist. They were in a face-off. His superior vampire strength didn't help when the water prevented him from getting a firm purchase on the floor. He was being pushed back.

"Run!" he ordered Eliza.

A loud crashing sound split the air around them and intense heat scorched the room. The water began to steam, bubble, and hiss around the siren and Mikhail. The whirlpool collapsed in on itself with a horrific grating noise. The room shook. Both Mikhail and the siren were thrown to the floor in a tangle of limbs. Mikhail's head met the marble floor with a thud. Trapped and dazed, Mikhail watched as the siren got back to his feet and with a cry of victory twisted Mikhail's wrist until the knife pressed against Mikhail's exposed throat. Mikhail pushed back and managed to move the siren enough to kick out. The bastard screamed in pain. The siren didn't stop yelling even when Mikhail finally flipped the intruder off of him. In fact, the sound became worse, and Mikhail stared in horror as the siren's skin bubbled and turned black until the siren burned to nothing in front of him. Within seconds, all that remained of the attacker was a charred mess on the floor. Bile rose in Mikhail's throat. He scooted back and away, moving rapidly.

What the fuck?

A small figure leapt at him, and he realized Eliza was sitting on him with her hands up and waving at something. A shadow. *Wings?* Mikhail blinked at the image of wings that spanned the entire bathroom and flickered with silver. Then he saw nothing more than the figure of a naked man in front of him; tall and broad with long gold hair and piercing silver eyes filled with icy control.

"Jin! No!" Eliza shouted.

"Step away, Your Highness," the man said firmly. *Your Highness?*

"He saved me," she said.

This wasn't right. Mikhail didn't need a child getting between him and whoever the hell it was with the hair and the eyes and the muscled body. He wasn't going to face death with a child as his shield. After pushing her off his lap, he levered himself to stand and shuddered as he kicked off parts of the charred siren that lay across his feet. He plucked his knife from the remains of a hand. He'd never seen anything that horrific, and part of him regretted that was the last thing he might see. Standing tall, he held up his knife in front of him and relaxed his stance.

Eliza moved swiftly to stand between them. Mikhail attempted to push her away again, but the little brat wouldn't move.

"No," she said. Mikhail wasn't entirely sure if she was talking to him or the other guy… the naked one.

Speaking of Mr. Naked, the man stepped forward. "Princess, we can't have any loose ends."

"No. You'll not kill him. He's a good vampire. He saved me."

The naked man stood absolutely still for a moment, then, as if he'd come to a decision, he bowed his head. With a flick of his fingers, he was clothed in soft, dark leather pants and a flowing sapphire silk shirt which covered the acres of exposed golden skin and muscles. Mikhail squelched his instinctive protest.

"We have to go," the now-dressed intruder said firmly.

"I'm not leaving," Eliza snapped. "We owe this house a payment, Jin."

Mikhail glanced from Eliza to Formerly Naked Guy and shook his head to clear it. A payment? What was Eliza? Who was this man? Had he really seen wings? Maybe he hadn't. Obviously he wasn't going to be doing any more fighting, considering this *Jin* was now pacing the short distance between the charred siren and the melted sink.

"Where have you been?" Jin asked Eliza as he walked. Mikhail stepped closer to the bathroom doorway to give the big guy some more room and be ready to escape.

"I was kidnapped. When I woke up, they used magic on me so I couldn't call the clutch."

"No other paranormal can use magic on you."

"They did."

Jin frowned. "Only another dragon—"

"I had to wait until there was no one in the house," Eliza interrupted.

"Dragon?" Mikhail said, his jaw falling open. Jin and Eliza both ignored him.

"Mikhail didn't leave," Eliza said. "Then the sirens came and we needed you."

Mikhail bristled despite the word dragon taking over his thoughts.

"I was doing fine," he said in his defense. "I didn't need him riding to the rescue." Mikhail pointed to Jin who ignored him.

"How did you get away?" Jin asked, stopping his frantic trek across the room to pierce her with his silver gaze.

"I was rescued by a demon, a wolf, a vampire and a human. They brought me here with the other children."

"Other children?" Jin looked confused.

Eliza shook her head. "They didn't take just me."

"Did they know?"

"No."

Did who know what? The kidnappers? Was Jin asking if the people who had snatched her knew what Eliza was? Jin called her princess, but a princess of what? Like he was a siren prince? *Had been a siren prince*, he corrected himself.

Something caught his attention in the pool of water in the hall. Mikhail walked over to discover the small glass box that the first siren had been holding. He picked it up and turned it over in his hands thoughtfully. A simple clear cube, like a solid lump of glass or something similar, lay hard and cold on his palm. Abruptly, Jin appeared beside Mikhail, his hand closing around Mikhail's.

An electric spark snapped between them. Mikhail nearly dropped the cube before Jin had a good hold of it. Mikhail looked up in shock, the connection had sent tingles throughout his entire body.

"Where did this come from?" Jin asked. His narrow-eyed gaze swept Mikhail as if his face would reveal the answers.

"One of the sirens had it," Mikhail replied. He didn't have anything to hide, unlike his guests.

And there was that spark again. For a second, Jin stared deep into his eyes. This close, Mikhail could see the purest silver irises and the question in them. Mikhail frowned as he focused his gaze lower, at the pulse in Jin's throat. He suddenly, inexplicably, wanted to sink his incisors into Jin's vein and drink his fill. Startled, he looked back up at Jin and allowed the man to gently prize the cube from his fingers. Jin held it out in front of him on his open palm. They both peered down at it.

Eliza stood on her tiptoes to get a better look and gasped. "It's a Draigbron." She sounded surprised. "I've never actually seen one before. That explains them tracking me down."

"Where did sirens get a Draigbron?" Jin asked urgently. "And how did they know to track you?"

"What's a Draigbron?" Mikhail asked. Could it be something that caused the electricity to arc between him and Jin? And why did that word sound like dragon, and who the hell was going to answer a damn question in all of this?

Jin glanced at him, then at Eliza. When Eliza nodded, with some unspoken agreement between them, Jin sighed.

"A dragon's heart."

Chapter Two

SAM STORMED INTO THE HOUSE, NOT CARING IF BOB followed him or not.

"Sam!" Bob shouted.

"I'm not talking to you!" Sam snarled. No more. He'd had enough of the vampire's antics.

"You can't blame me for the last one," Bob protested. "You nixed every school we went to."

"I certainly can." Sam spun around and folded his arms in front of his chest as he faced his lover. "You didn't stick up for me."

"Because you're unreasonable!" Bob yelled.

"I was not being unreasonable," Sam protested through gritted teeth.

"Sam, I liked that last school. Can I please go there?" Mal's small voice broke into their fight.

"They ban humans! I'm not going to pay to put you in a school that wouldn't take me!" Sam scowled.

"No, they would've taken you because of your affinity for paranormals. You weren't listening to the headmistress," Bob argued.

"Maybe it was the 'no humans' sign that threw me off," Sam countered.

Bob rolled his eyes. "Don't let your personal feelings prevent you from giving Mal a good education. They said they had no problems with you being a participating parent. I'll even foot the bill."

Sam thought about kicking his lover, very hard.

Bob wisely stepped back out of range.

Sometimes it paid to have a boyfriend who could read his mind. Sam turned to face Mal. "You really liked it there?"

Mal nodded, her thin face lit with excitement. "One of the other kids is like me. I could feel him."

Sam bit his lip. He knew how important it would be for Mal to be among others who might understand her even a little bit. The school Mal liked served not only as a school but also as a home for these children. If she attended, she would live there and only visit Sam and Bob for holidays. Sam had to admit that part of his reluctance had to do with losing a daughter he'd only just obtained.

"If I register you there, you have to promise to tell me the second you have any issues." Sam tried to convey the seriousness of his request. He wouldn't have Mal bullied.

"She'll be fine," Bob promised.

Sam looked from Mal to Bob and back again. He hated the idea of sending Mal to a school that held such prejudices. However, since he also had once only wanted humans coming to his practice, he couldn't hold onto his anger. He couldn't be that much of a hypocrite.

"Fine but Bob, you're paying," Sam acceded.

"Yay!" Mal threw herself into Sam's arms. "Thank you, Sam. Thank you. Thank you."

Sam awkwardly patted her back. He'd never be good at this father thing anyway. Why did he even try?

Mal released him. "You're an excellent father," she argued. "I've never had anyone care so much before. You turned down three schools because the kids looked unhappy. At least at this one, they were well taken care of, right?"

Sam nodded. He had to remember to be careful what he thought in his daughter's presence. She would know if he was being negative. Despite the school's arguably poor discriminative practices, the kids at the last school had all appeared to be playing and laughing like regular kids.

"I suppose."

"Sam! I'm glad you're here!" Mikhail raced down the stairs followed by a big man with long golden hair and the little girl they'd rescued.

"What happened?" Sam asked, keeping a cautious eye on the stranger.

"I'm Ryujin," the tall man said formally. "But you can call me Jin."

Mikhail nodded. "So this is Jin and our girl's name is Eliza. Eliza is a dragon princess and is in danger of being recaptured by the sirens. We need to get her back home." Mikhail said this so matter-of-factly that Sam wouldn't have reacted quite so badly had Mikhail not been covered in blood. A quick assessment showed it probably wasn't Mikhail's…

Hang on… Dragons?

"Dragons don't come this far away from the mountains." Sam frowned at the trio. How did he not know about dragons visiting before? They were definitely not in any of his training notebooks.

"You are the most unprepared sleuth I've ever met," Bob said.

"Hey, I've cracked two cases so far." Not on his own and not without mishap, but they had ended well.

Bob shook his head.

Wait a minute! What did Mikhail mean? Home? Home where?

"We? What do you mean *we* need to get her back home?" Sam frowned at Mikhail. The siren-vampire generally had a good head on his shoulders, but, right then, his eyes were a bit wild and desperate.

Bob turned to Jin. "If you are her guardian, why do we need to get involved?"

Sam had to admit he wondered about that too.

Jin growled. "Because you're detectives and we need to hire you. We have to figure out who kidnapped Eliza. She was taken while sleeping and saw nothing, and it could be that one of our own is involved."

"Sirens," Sam said. "It was sirens. We solved that one." He turned to Bob for support, but Bob was talking to Jin.

"Why don't you call your own kind to protect her?" Bob asked. "Surely the best thing to protect a dragon is another dragon?"

A chill went down Sam's spine at the thought of dragon shifters invading his home before he could get Eliza out of his house. The wolves had been bad enough. He'd rather help the dragon himself than allow more into his house.

"Exactly how many dragons are there?" Sam asked cautiously. "And did no one hear me mention the sirens?"

Jin ignored Sam and instead focused on Bob's question. His mouth twisted into a bitter smile. "I don't know who to trust, and I won't, until I see the entire clutch at home. I'm worried about calling on the wrong people to return Eliza to her father."

"Wait, Sam can protect me, and find out who did this," Eliza said suddenly.

What? Sam frowned at the little girl, wondering why she

thought he could do anything when there were much stronger paranormals in the room.

Mal stepped in front of Sam. "Sam's *my* daddy!"

Eliza growled, showing off an impressive set of incisors.

"Girls!" Bob snapped. He moved to stand between them.

"Mal, we're going to set you up with the school tomorrow," Bob said. "Eliza, we'll accompany you home, Mikhail can help, and Sam will track down who did this."

"I will?" Sam asked.

"I'm helping?" Mikhail asked. Sam looked at the vampire-siren and guessed Mikhail's wide eyed expression was similar to his own.

Bob ignored the interruptions from both Sam and Mikhail. "But your bodyguard here has to realize that the dragons will be in our debt." He folded his arms across his chest as if daring anyone to argue with his statement.

"Why do you think we need this human, Sam?" Jin asked Eliza.

"Can't you feel it?" Eliza asked in a soft, wondrous tone. "He's been faery touched."

JIN STARED at the human for a long moment. He didn't appear to be overly remarkable. Rather handsome for one of their species, with kind brown eyes and rumpled blond hair—not as beautiful as the siren-vampire from the bathroom but attractive in his own way nonetheless. From the narrowed-eyed look the other vampire gave him, Sam evidently belonged to Bob.

Using his other sight, Jin examined Sam again. He couldn't prevent the gasp from escaping. Sam glowed with an unearthly light. The prints of other paranormals who'd crossed his path brushed across his aura like finger paints.

Streaks of color from a fae's blessing kiss, a demon's protection spell, a vampire's bonding mark, and a familiar's magic all swirled across Sam. The human had more magical touches than people who'd lived thousands of years. Jin saw tendrils of a connection to a wolf shifter, but he couldn't pin down the color. Across all the connections, a strong swathe of magical energy twisted through the entire mass.

"You are just a human, right?" Jin asked.

Sam rolled his eyes. "What do you mean 'just a human', and why does everyone keep asking that?"

Jin turned his attention to Bob who shook his head. He quickly abandoned that line of questioning. If the human's mate didn't want to discuss Sam's magical energy, Jin wouldn't bring it up again. He didn't need to stir up extra trouble. He had a job to do—returning the princess safely home. He didn't have time to waste talking. If Eliza said Sam was what she needed, it wasn't his place to argue. The more people on their side to get her safely home the better.

Jin cleared his throat before continuing. "We would be delighted to have you accompany us." Eliza beamed up at him. "The clutch will, of course, pay restitution for your bathroom and your time."

"Wait," Sam said. "What do you mean pay for my bathroom? What happened to my bathroom?" Without waiting for a reply, Sam stomped through the group and headed upstairs.

"Now you did it," Bob scolded.

Jin shrugged. It wasn't like Sam wouldn't find out about the damage eventually.

Mikhail shoved him. And while it felt good to have the gorgeous vamp's hands on him, he wasn't that impressed with what Mikhail said.

"If Sam isn't happy, you'd best start running, dragon."

What could a human do to him, even a gifted one?

"What the hell happened to my house?" Sam shrieked from above.

The vampire girl's eyes glowed. "You upset Sam!" she snapped.

Jin shook his head. It wasn't his fault that Sam's bathroom was nothing more than a vista of melted metal and smashed porcelain. Bob placed a hand on the little vampire's shoulder, stopping her from moving closer. Jin was pleased. He didn't want to have to hurt her if she attacked him. A vampire, especially a child, was no match for a dragon.

A low growling sound and a pop of electricity heralded the appearance of a familiar. A shiver of fear coursed through Jin as the cat's eyes narrowed and fixed on him. A small vampire might not worry him, but dragonkin knew better than to mess with familiars. Their wild magic could cause unimaginable harm. He'd heard stories of old dragons going mad when they heard the words in their thoughts. Familiars often lived to be thousands of years old and made dangerous enemies.

"Be kind to my human," the creature warned. *"I've made it my job to take care of those who harm him."*

Jin nodded. "I will," he said. He wasn't going to argue. He valued his life.

The black cat flicked its tail before sauntering from the entryway.

Mikhail looked at him strangely. "You spoke to Smudge? You can hear the cat?"

Jin nodded. "It's a dragonkin thing."

Mikhail laughed, and Jin stiffened. Dragons were not to be laughed at.

"Smudge is very protective, but you're the first outside of

Sam to hear him talk. Let's go check on Sam, and we can explain what happened."

"Let's." Jin wasn't sure where the familiar had gone, and he didn't want to be there when the small beast returned. Even the dragon king had less scary eyes than that little cat.

He ushered Eliza up with him—no way was he taking his eyes off of her. They joined Sam in the bathroom, and Jin couldn't believe how devastated the sort-of-human looked. It was only a bathroom, and people's lives had been saved by the actions of himself and the siren-vamp.

"I'll never be able to rent it now," Sam said, shaking his head at the mess.

"We'll pay to fix it," Jin assured him. "I can give you gold."

Sam looked at him with a resigned expression on his face. "What happened to my waterfall? And my whirlpool."

"I closed the portal after Jin arrived," Eliza said. "More sirens could've come through if I didn't."

"So, how did you come through the portal?" Mikhail asked Jin.

Jin turned to face the gorgeous siren-vamp. He'd been struck by the man's beauty the first time he saw him, wrestling with the other siren on the floor. Up close, he looked and smelled like the kind of supernatural Jin wanted to add to his collection of jewels and gold. To wake up every day and see the beautiful sea-green eyes staring up at him would be better than waking to a pan full of rubies and emeralds.

"I could feel my connection with Eliza when she came close to the portal. I followed my instincts and entered through an underground river. It is better that it no longer exists—anyone could've come through there," he told Sam.

"I had no idea it was dangerous. It was so pretty." Sam continued to stare at his ruined bathroom.

"I know a very good handyman," Jin promised.

Sam sighed. "Okay."

"Why can't you just create another portal and take Eliza home?" Mikhail asked.

"Portals are tricky and, although dragonkin can use them, we can't create our own," Jin replied. He hated telling Mikhail some of their secrets, but he needed to explain why he couldn't risk taking Eliza back without support. "I'd take her back with me alone, but the Draigbron might still be calling to anyone who knows how to connect to it. It will take more than me to get the princess home safe."

"What's a Draigbron?" Sam asked.

Jin held up the cube in his hand. "This. We call it a Draigbron, but it is really the magical essence of a dragon who has died. If I remember my studies, this one belongs to Eliza's great-great-grandmother."

"That thing used to be a dragon shifter?" Sam's appalled expression had Jin rushing to explain. He didn't want the human so distressed that he called off his help.

"Magical energy never really dies. When a dragon's life ends, the essence of his or her power consolidates into one of these cubes. It can work as a homing beacon on any of the dead dragon's descendants, and sometimes a relative can also use it to access the cube's magic. However, not every relative can access every Draigbron. They need a special genetic chemistry, if you will." Jin hoped he'd explained it well enough.

Sam nodded his understanding. "Where did you get this one?"

"From the sirens. Which means a dragonkin is working with them. It's the only way they could have gotten one." The betrayal hurt. To think one of their own would work with the sea spawn made Jin's chest ache. "This is why Eliza says we need your help. We don't know who to trust."

Jin held his breath while he waited for a reply. He hoped both vampires and even the blessed human would agree to accompany him. He had no doubt the vamps would be able to help during any battle. He had doubts about the human, Sam, but he could tell that none of the others would accompany him without Sam's agreement. Certainly Bob, the vampire, wouldn't move forward without his mate.

"Where do dragon shifters live?" Sam finally asked with a sigh, after what seemed like ages.

"In the Fire Heart Mountains. The entire range is home to our kind," Jin replied.

"Wow, that's a large space," Sam said in a surprised tone.

"We need to be spread out. Dragons require large territories to roam," Jin explained, even though there wasn't really time for small talk. They should be moving and soon.

"How long will it take to get there?" Sam asked.

"Five hours by car," Jin said quickly. He didn't want them to think it would be an incredibly long journey. Back when they'd had to travel by foot, it had taken a while. Some places on the mountain were difficult to reach without wings but not impossible. Enough dragons had mated outside their species that land-based paths had needed to be cut through the hard rock.

No one spoke as Sam's gaze swept across the group. "We can leave tomorrow after we drop off Mal."

"You have to ignore your own needs," Jin began.

"No, I have to ignore the fact that marauding dragons might attack our home," Sam snapped. "Our daughter is more important."

Jin snorted his disapproval. "We wait here and everyone might die."

Sam crossed his hands over his chest. He wasn't budging one inch on this and Jin could recognize stubborn pig-headedness when he saw it.

"Nevertheless, that is how long you will wait if you want us to go with you," Sam replied. He still looked dazed. "Mal is important to us and we want her settled. Your dragon princess will be safe here."

Sam turned and walked out of the bathroom without another word. Bob and Mal quickly followed him.

Jin tilted his head as he tried to figure out what had just happened.

Mikhail sighed. "Don't try to figure Sam out. It'll just drive you crazy. With Sam, it's better to go with the flow."

"What is he?" Jin asked as soon as he was sure Sam was out of hearing range.

Mikhail poked Jin in the side. "Don't mention anything about him not being completely human. He's sensitive about his abilities." There was a lot of affection in Mikhail's voice.

"What are his abilities?" Jin asked. "Could he turn? Could he be dangerous?"

Mikhail's answer sounded vague. "His abilities keep evolving."

"I'm tired," Eliza complained.

"Is there someplace she can nap?" Jin asked. Breathing fire took a lot out of a dragonkin, especially one as young as Eliza. She needed rest followed by a large, protein-rich meal. "I can stay outside her door and guard her."

Mikhail shook his head. "Teddy can watch her."

"Who's Teddy?" Jin couldn't help but think that this was the strangest place he'd ever visited.

"The house ghost," Mikhail explained. "Teddy!"

A transparent shape drifted through the wall. Jin thought the ghost's aura had a sad edge. He wondered how the young man had died.

"What do you want, Mikhail?" Teddy said tiredly. "I was reading."

Jin couldn't believe the ghost hadn't heard any of the commotion in the bathroom. Was reading really that important?

"I want you to watch over Eliza while she sleeps. Yell if she needs anything or if someone disturbs her."

Teddy turned a listless gaze to the dragon child. "All right."

Jin didn't quite trust the ghost, but if Mikhail believed the spook would guard Eliza, he didn't want to cause problems by objecting. He could grab a spot to sleep outside her door after he checked out the house for security. He needed to set wards and protections to make sure they were shielded from their enemies. He hoped whoever had used the Draigbron to track down Eliza had somehow worked alone and hadn't made Eliza's position general knowledge. At least other sirens wouldn't be unable to reach her again with the portal shut.

His mind spun with questions. Who wanted Eliza? For what purpose? Dragon kidnappings were rare, simply because dragons generally kept themselves away from most of the world.

Staying would also give him alone time with Mikhail. The man smelled incredible, a divine combination of sea salt and blood…

His attention snapped to his companion.

Blood!

"You were cut!" Jin exclaimed. He didn't know why, but

the thought of Mikhail bleeding caused sudden panic to race through him.

"I'm fine. I'm already healed." Sam and Bob appeared in the corridor again, and Jin was momentarily distracted. "Sam, do you mind if I use the other apartment to wash up?"

Sam shook his head. "No. That's fine. Do you want some clothes? I'm sure Bob has something you can wear."

Jin noticed Bob didn't object to Sam's confiscation of his wardrobe. The vampire's fond look at Sam pretty much conveyed his attitude toward the human. Whatever Sam wanted would be how things went. Jin knew he'd have to watch his step with Sam. It appeared he had some powerful allies.

"A change of clothes would be appreciated," Mikhail said.

"I'll get them." Bob left quickly, presumably to fetch Mikhail something to wear.

Sam laughed. "He's worried I'll pick out his favorite outfit or something. I'm not to be trusted with his wardrobe."

The human didn't appear overly concerned with his lover's worries about clothing. Sam darted a glance between Jin and Mikhail. "I'll go make sure he finds something."

Sam vanished so quickly that Jin wondered for a bit if he'd really walked away.

They settled Eliza into the bed for her nap and left her under ghostly supervision.

"Why do you think the sirens were after her? And who do you suspect gave the sirens the dragon heart?" Mikhail asked Jin when they were finally alone.

Jin could think of a lot of things to do with the stunning siren-vampire besides answer questions. The dragon just beneath his skin urged him to lick and savor Mikhail's body.

Maybe he'd need a friend to scrub his back in the shower later?

"I don't know. Those are things I need to find out."

He approached Mikhail, the attraction between them flared hotter than a dragon's flame. He stepped back in shock. His dragon might be urging him to explore his connection with Mikhail, but he had duties to perform before he could strip the man down and do a personal taste test.

"I need to check the perimeter," he said, quickly adding more space between them.

Mikhail nodded. "I'll guide you around."

Obviously for Mikhail, showering and changing clothes was secondary to assisting Jin, and for that Jin felt an uncommon warmth inside his heart. Together, they traced the extent of the property, from side to side and from basement to roof, until Jin was finally happy that he could defend against any and all attacks. It was as they were climbing the basement steps back into the main reception that something occurred to him.

"You pushed Eliza away when she tried to protect you. She's a dragon princess and very strong. You could have let her save you from the sirens."

"I didn't know she was a dragon shifter, did I?" Mikhail said softly. "In my mind, she was a little girl and I wasn't going to let anyone hurt her."

"You're very brave." They closed the basement door, and Mikhail turned the large brass key in the lock until the door was firmly secured. When he spun around, he was yet again in Jin's space. The familiar spark between them intrigued Jin, and there was one thing he wanted to do.

"I have to kiss you, Mikhail. Please tell me my touch is welcome." Jin knew he sounded formal, but he was a dragon and he didn't know how to speak any other way. When a dragon courted, there were rules to be followed. What would Mikhail say?

"A kiss?" Mikhail questioned. Then he repeated it again. "A kiss."

"Just a kiss. I have to taste my mate."

Mikhail frowned, and Jin wished he hadn't mentioned the mate word, despite what his dragon-self was telling him to say.

"What about your duty to the princess?" Mikhail reminded Jin.

Jin shut his eyes and took a step away. "You're right," he said.

"You can't let him go."

Jin jumped at the words intruding into his mind. He hadn't even seen the cat enter the room.

"What do you mean?" he asked.

"You know as well as I do that he will complete you. I will watch the sleeping child with the ghost. You stay here and stake your claim."

Jin glanced at Mikhail, who was still frowning but this time at the familiar perched on the bottom step, twitching its tail.

"I take it Smudge is talking to you again?" Mikhail asked, bemused.

"He says he will watch Eliza with the ghost," Jin explained. He felt it wise to leave off the staking his claim business.

"Just so we can kiss?" Mikhail's doubtful expression had Jin rushing to reassure him.

"Yes." Jin avoided any other conversation by grabbing Mikhail's hand and pulling him into the closest room. The space smelled musty and old, and a quick scan revealed tables of paperwork, files, folders, rolled maps, and big filing cabinets. Surely they were unlikely to be disturbed in here.

"You really trust the cat to watch Eliza?" Mikhail asked.

Jin didn't even have to think about his answer. "With my life."

"I don't understand that. Smudge may be a familiar, but at the end of the day, he's a cat. What can Smudge do against— umph."

Jin stepped in to stop Mikhail talking and stole a sudden kiss, before immediately backing away. The touch against the siren-vamp's lips was as alluring as fire to him. Mikhail looked shocked and dazed and placed the index finger of his right hand on his mouth.

"Are you well?" Jin asked formally. Lesser beings than he had been known to expire after a dragon's kiss. Not every supernatural could calm the flame inside a dragonkin.

"That wasn't a proper kiss," Mikhail murmured.

"Would you like a proper kiss?" Jin hated that he sounded so needy. What he wouldn't do to have Mikhail naked and writhing under him in less than ten seconds.

Now he just waited for the answer.

Chapter Three

WHERE HAD THE ALL-ACTION DRAGONKIN GONE? INSTEAD, Jin stood in front of Mikhail looking uncertain. Mikhail wasn't stupid. He'd felt the spark between them whenever they got close, but he was prepared to wait until everything went back to normal before he even thought of having a night of fun with the sexy dragon. He was ignoring the fact that he'd heard the word 'mate' and all the resulting issues that came with it. That was such an outdated concept, and it didn't apply to him. He just wanted sex.

He didn't for one minute believe that a crossbreed like himself had a fated mate, or an instant bond or anything like Sam and Bob. But he did believe that there was definitely heat between him and Jin. He focused on the fact that some part of him needed the dragon's touch. Now.

"Yes," he said quickly.

In an instant, Jin was up in his space and the ridiculously strong dragon lifted him off the floor. Jin positioned him on one of the map tables and nudged his knees until Mikhail widened the space between his legs and Jin could fit between them. Cradling his face, Jin kissed him gently, then deepened the kiss. Lust sparked inside Mikhail, and he linked his hands behind Jin's back to hold them groin to groin. The feel of the dragon against him was intoxicating, and he wanted to touch skin. What did dragons do during sex? Mikhail released his grip and pushed a hand between them, sliding into Jin's pants. He closed his fingers around Jin's cock and there… That was a pretty impressive cock, but nothing he couldn't handle.

Jin moaned low in his throat at the touch, and Mikhail felt heady with the power he held over the dragon. Jin had begun by showing Mikhail careful consideration, but now he was frantic with need. Firmly, Mikhail pumped his hand a few times and twisted his thumb over the tip to slide through the pre-cum that collected there. Like that, with the back of his hand moving against his own cock at the same time, it was inevitable that he would peak soon. Jin cursed as he released the kiss, and Mikhail stared into silver eyes that glowed with flecks of orange. Fire glowed in the depths of them— fascinating.

"M-m-mate," Jin stuttered, then lost it, steamy hot and wet into Mikhail's hand, with Mikhail following close after.

Mikhail remained unconvinced about the mate thing and he ignored the insistent press of that same word inside his head. He'd known the dragon for only a few hours—he shouldn't be feeling like he wanted forever. Should he?

Jin stepped back and gestured at Mikhail's clothes. "I'm sorry," he said simply.

"I needed a shower anyway," Mikhail said. Then inspiration hit him. "You're all messed up as well."

Jin glanced down at his pants with confusion written on his face. Then puzzlement gave way to a shy smile and yet another layer of protection smashed around Mikhail's heart.

"You want to have a shower together?" Jin asked hopefully.

Mikhail answered the best way he could, by copying how Jin had manhandled him into the file room. He tugged Jin up one flight of stairs and through the spare apartment he was using to the other bathroom. Jin pulled the door shut and locked it.

Mikhail fiddled with the controls, turned to encourage Jin to undress. But Jin was already well ahead of Mikhail. Naked and proud, he was a sight for sore eyes. Muscled, big, and just ever so sexy, the big dragon was fisting himself and already had an impressive erection. Mikhail stripped in seconds and tugged his dragon lover into the shower. The water was hot, and for a short while, they both allowed it to run over them. It was a hundred kinds of awkward in the small area, but it appeared that Jin had an idea of how to handle the issue. With swift movements, he had Mikhail in his arms, encouraging him to wrap his legs around him until there was no space between them.

Mikhail had never had a lover who could hold him, so solid and right. They kissed for a long time until Mikhail lost track of everything except the feel of Jin's clever mouth and the need for more.

"One day, I want to be inside you," Jin growled against Mikhail's throat.

"One day?" Mikhail asked. Why were they waiting? He must have said something out loud, or maybe his expression gave it away that he was impatient for more.

"Tradition. Love. Mates. We need to do this right."

"And right isn't acting on what we both feel?" Mikhail asked carefully. He knew very little about the sex life of a dragon, and even less about being the person attached to Jin's label of *mate*.

Jin buried his face against Mikhail's throat. "You are worth more to me than just taking you now. I can't just fuck you like this, without proper steps. There is ritual to observe."

Mikhail couldn't help the pouty expression he knew he presented. "Let me down," he ordered. Jin did as he was instructed, but instead of standing, Mikhail maneuvered until he was on his knees between Jin's spread legs. He didn't ask permission before closing his mouth around the dragon's cock and showed him exactly what they *could* do while they waited for the main event. He spent a long time teasing and exploring with his tongue, tasting every inch of the impressive size. Jin buried his hands into Mikhail's hair and gripped tight even as he cursed and hissed above him. He was reduced to pleading in what Mikhail imagined was dragon tongue, and, with a roar, he erupted down Mikhail's throat.

Mikhail abruptly felt like the most powerful man in the entire world as he swallowed every drop and hummed his approval. With his hand fisting his own cock, his release soon followed Jin's. When the dragon helped him stand, Mikhail realized he had no strength left in his legs. Jin scooped him up into an awkward lift in a huge fluffy towel. Mikhail simply smiled as he was carried to the bed. He could get used to this.

His last thought, as they snuggled close, was that he really needed to look into how the dragon's mating customs affected him. In the warm afterglow, he imagined, if only for the night, that even a mixed blood like him might have a chance to be worthy of a dragon's love.

SAM WAS close to completely losing all of his patience. Not only did he and Bob need to get Mal to school for her first day, but she needed enough supplies to keep her comfortable for the next five weeks. With the car finally packed tight, they were ready to leave, but no one could find Bob.

"Where are you?" he thought as he climbed into the driver's seat.

"I'll be there in five," Bob thought back.

"What are you doing?"

"Packing for our journey. I can't find my blue pants."

Sam sighed. He loved Bob, he really did, but at times like this, he could throttle the freaking vampire. *"I'm leaving with or without you,"* he ended the conversation firmly.

"I'm here," Bob announced breathlessly. He was attempting to convey 'sorry' with a contrite expression, and Sam shook his head at the blatant attempt at innocence. There was nothing innocent about his Bob.

Jin and Mikhail watched from the doorway, and Sam couldn't fail to see the dragon shifter's hand on Mikhail's shoulder. Goodness only knew what was happening between the two of them. The dragon looked possessive—Mikhail just appeared worried. Maybe he should get Bob to ask Mikhail what was going on.

"He wouldn't like that," Bob replied to his thought with one of his own. *"I'm not getting a good feeling about them, but once a dragon decides they have found their mate…"* His thoughts trailed away, and he shrugged. Sam sighed. He would never understand paranormals and their whole fated mates thing. Although, glancing at Bob as he buckled himself in, he knew he had found his partner for life, despite Bob's inability to ever be early for anything. So wasn't it actually true they had a fated mates kind of connection?

"I love you, Bob."

Bob patted his knee. *"I love you too."*

Finally, with all three of them in the car, they took the main road out of End Street. In just a little over an hour, they were at the gates of the school. Mal had been unusually quiet, and Sam worried the entire journey about whether they were doing the right thing.

"Maybe we should look into home-schooling our little vampire?"

"No," Bob thought immediately.

"But—"

"No. She needs to learn more than we can ever show her."

Sam subsided into trying *not* to think about anything to do with Mal. He felt slightly better when, as soon as the car stopped in the parking lot, Mal's mood lifted. The three of them climbed out of the car, and Sam surveyed the old structure that looked as if it had been there for centuries. Inside was modern and new, but the outside spoke of history.

"Mal. Remember. You don't have to do this," Sam said one final time. "We could find a school closer to home." This was hard, having to leave Mal. She'd only been with them two weeks, but he'd grown really fond of her.

"I want to come here, Sam," she said firmly. "I told you there's someone else here like me and I'm really excited. I have things to do here. Important things." The last part she added with a mysterious smile.

Sam pulled her in for a hug, which she allowed. "Bob is taking you in," he said gently.

Bob glanced at him quickly. "I am?"

"I'm not going inside," Sam said firmly.

"Why? Is it because of the ban on human children?"

Sam shook his head. He couldn't explain why he wasn't going in, because he didn't know. It wasn't just that human children weren't welcome at the school, although that didn't help. There was something off about the way he felt when he'd stood in the atrium on their last visit. Like his head buzzed and was too full. No doubt having a head filled with chattering adolescents was some freaky gift he had been given at some point in the last few weeks. What was the use of a gift like that?

"*Are you okay?*" Bob thought. "*I'm worried. You look pale.*"

"*I'm fine. Do this for me, Bob.*"

BOTH MEN WERE quiet on the way back. Bob had come out of the school looking sad, and Sam felt guilty. He should have been able to go inside. What had Mal meant when she had said she had things to do in the school? His mind wandered over possible scenarios, which ran from Mal murdering everyone in their beds with her vampire teeth, to Mal volunteering to clean blackboards.

"Not all vampires are murderers, Sam," Bob snapped.

"I didn't... I wasn't..." Sam defended, then stopped bothering. Sometimes it would be really nice not to have Bob in his head.

They reached home to find Jin, Mikhail, and Eliza all waiting inside, looking eager to move on. Loading bags of essentials into the trunk, they decided that Mikhail and Bob would go in the backseat with Eliza. Jin, by virtue of the fact that he was the biggest, would sit in the passenger seat of Sam's Ford.

Sam stood in reception and called out to Teddy, who didn't immediately appear. Instead, it was Smudge who padded down the stairs, then sat on the bottom step looking up at him with sphinx-like green eyes.

"*Take special care in the mountains, Sam.*"

"*Will you stay here then?*" He wasn't sure how familiars

worked. Were they not supposed to stay with their... well, whatever he was?

"I will watch the house. Bob will watch you."

"Okay. So, um... bye then. If you need me, you have my cell number." Now that was a stupid thing to say. Given that the cat could transport itself wherever it wanted, Sam imagined a phone wasn't needed. Anyway, cats didn't have opposable thumbs to hold a phone. And Teddy couldn't help —his hand would go through the cell. And the stone gargoyle would simply crush the phone...

He pulled himself out of his thoughts and worries. He had to trust that Smudge could look after himself and the house.

Smudge, probably having heard all of his thoughts, said nothing back. Instead, he twitched his tail and lifted a paw to lick at it. That was the image Sam was left with. Not of an all-powerful and ancient magic familiar, but of a house cat licking his paw.

When they drove away from the house, Sam couldn't shake the feeling of dread.

When Bob and Eliza started singing in the back, the fear only worsened. He loved Bob and if anything happened to him...

Bob met his eyes in the mirror and smiled. Sam heard his lover's words in his head and it calmed him a little.

"Everything will be okay, Sam, you'll see..."

Chapter Four

Jin sat at an angle so he could watch Mikhail out of the corner of his eye. He'd never thought he'd find his mate and certainly not in a vampire-siren hybrid. Mikhail shone brighter than any of the jewels in Jin's hoard and was twice as pretty.

Nervousness over how the others in his clutch would accept his mate caused Jin to shiver and his wings threatened to extend. He couldn't help thinking they wouldn't be as enchanted with Mikhail as he was. Dragons as a species didn't approve of vampires, and throwing in Mikhail's siren blood didn't help matters. Although humans and other shifters were acceptable mates, rarely did dragons go for the biters or the swimmers.

Jin shoved those concerns out of the window. He refused to be thwarted from claiming his mate.

Determined, he gave his attention to the driver. Sam's constant annoyance with *his* Bob, *his* mate, amused Jin. The connection between the human and the vampire had strong threads of love and devotion with a white stream as a sign the gods approved twisting between them. Jin had rarely seen two people so properly matched.

Bob had an air of amused affection around him, but when he watched Sam, Jin could see the strong determination in the man to never, ever let his mate go. Bob might appear relaxed in the back of the car, singing with the dragon princess, but his aura gave no room for doubt. No one had better mess with Bob's human, or there would be hell to pay.

Jin had a lot of time to contemplate what he wanted with Mikhail, as driving up to the Fire Heart Mountains took longer than he had expected. He'd never taken the long way home before. Flying or portal travel were his preferred methods.

His thoughts went from Mikhail to Eliza and back to the last dragon council meeting he'd attended. So many from the clutch had been distressed at the loss of the dragon princess, but Jin had sensed that a lot of the emotion was forced. With the princess out of the way there was one less obstacle to the throne. Although the throne wasn't strictly passed through the royal line, the fates general favored those of the king's blood to lead the dragons. He wondered how many of the dragons who'd proclaimed anguish at the princess's disappearance would be pleased that she had been found. Some of them had already started forming small cliques and could be found in meetings discussing who could possibly show the marks of the chosen heir should the King die; like Eliza was already dead. As if some of them knew more than they were letting on. "Stop worrying, Jin," Eliza said from the backseat.

"What makes you think I'm worrying?" Jin wished he had his tail. At least then he'd have something to play with while he fretted.

"You always worry," Eliza said simply.

"Humph," he muttered. A spurt of steam drifted from his

nostrils as his banked fire flickered. He ruthlessly fought it back. His human form couldn't tolerate the flame, unlike his dragon scales. The delicate nature of his human shape always set him on edge. Without fangs, claws, and fire, he always felt naked and vulnerable.

His gaze darted back to Mikhail only to find his stare returned.

Mikhail had a curious expression on his face, and his ocean-colored eyes glowed slightly in the bright afternoon sun. What was Mikhail thinking?

Jin didn't get a chance to ask.

"Let's stop for a minute and stretch our legs." Sam pulled the car over to a roadside convenience store.

From Jin's estimation, they were only halfway through the trip. He didn't want to stop, but he understood that humans needed breaks more than paras. Sam got out of the car. When Jin walked around, he saw Sam stretch his back and a series of pops crackled from him. He waited for a moment to see if perhaps Sam was a shape changer about to shift forms.

After Sam did nothing else of note, Jin headed for Mikhail.

"Why does his spine make those noises?" he whispered to his mate. He dipped his head low so he could sniff Mikhail's delicious scent.

Mikhail shoved him away. "Humans aren't as flexible as paras. His muscles tire if he's in the same position for so long."

Jin felt a small amount of horror for his new friend. To be so fragile and not even have a second self to protect you must be a horrible burden to bear. "Poor man," he muttered sympathetically.

Mikhail snorted. "I wouldn't let Sam hear you say that.

He's kind of sensitive about his human status, especially since none of us think he's purely human."

"Ah." Jin's concern for his new friend faded a bit. "Well, at least Bob will watch over him."

"Yes, there is that."

Jin watched Bob saunter over to his mate and wrap an arm around Sam's waist before yanking the smaller man into his arms. Jin looked away when they began kissing. Dragons weren't big on privacy, but somehow the intimacy in the way that the vampire embraced his human held more sexual punch than watching full-on sex.

"They are well matched."

"I know," Mikhail said, keeping his gaze on the pair. "It's stunning watching them together."

Jin hissed. "How much have you watched?"

He hadn't thought Bob the type to share his mate.

"Hmm? Oh, just kissing. Bob is surprisingly discreet. Sirens have sex in groups all the time, but vampires are more reserved about their private affairs."

The thought of Mikhail stripping naked before others made Jin's gums tingle and his fangs threaten to descend.

"Have you participated in these orgies?" Jin asked in a gravelly voice.

Mikhail turned his attention to Jin. "Yes, of course. I am part siren. I didn't come to you a virgin, dragon-man. I'm not ashamed of my past, and I won't pretend to be to make you feel better either."

Rage rushed through Jin at the image in his head of others touching his mate.

"Hey, shhh... No need to dragon out," Mikhail soothed. He petted Jin's skin, rubbing fingers up and down across Jin's arms, his neck, and sliding them playfully across Jin's ears.

Anger washed away beneath the tidal wave of instant desire. Unable to resist his mate, Jin wrapped a hand around the back of Mikhail's neck and pulled him closer. He pressed his mouth hard against Mikhail's, demanding entry. He would burn away the residue of any other man who took a fraction of Mikhail's devotion away. No other lover would be able to compete for Mikhail's love. The vamp-siren was his!

Mine! His dragon-self roared in agreement.

Mikhail jerked back. His wet lips shone in the sunlight. "I heard that!" His eyes widened with surprise.

"Heard what?" Jin asked.

"Your dragon." Mikhail slid his hands across Jin's chest. "I heard it talk to me."

Jin shrugged. *Surely he's heard shifters before?* "Can't vamps hear other people's thoughts?"

Mikhail shrugged. "Shifters are usually harder to listen in on. I couldn't hear yours until right now."

"My dragon wanted to talk to you. Dragons aren't like other shifters. We aren't humans who turn into dragons. We are dragons who transform into humans. Our natural state is our beast." Jin re-ran the statement through his head as he made sure he had said it correctly before nodding that he had.

"So I'm bonding with your beast?" Mikhail asked.

"In essence. I mean, when we have sex, it will be in human form, but our spiritual connection is more from man to beast than man to man. Does that make sense?" Jin knew he wasn't conveying things like he should. Frustration bubbled up inside him. He didn't want to lose Mikhail, but he wouldn't lie to him either. Other paras might shy away from such a visceral connection, but he hoped Mikhail would be stronger.

"Dragon shifters don't generally do well in the city?"

Mikhail asked. His sea-colored eyes conveyed a hidden message Jin didn't understand.

"Um... no, not usually." He examined his mate, waiting to figure out the real meaning behind the statement.

Mikhail said nothing. Instead, he frowned and pulled at his lower lip with a fang.

Jin puffed a bit of smoke into the air. "Will you just blurt it out? Dragons aren't good at reading subtlety. When we have something to say, we say it."

He knew sirens were of the sneaky sort, but he didn't want to say that to his half-siren mate because vampires weren't rumored to be any better. Mikhail might not identify with his siren roots because of whatever had happened in his past, but he couldn't change his nature. He waited as Mikhail sighed heavily.

"Where do you think we'll live if we are truly mates?" Mikhail asked.

That question had an easy answer. Jin was born to duty and he knew where he needed to be.

"I am a guard for Princess Eliza. I must live under the mountain with the royal family." Jin grimaced. "Assuming they let me keep my job after she was abducted."

"You weren't on duty that day," a small voice interrupted.

Jin turned to see that the princess had sneaked up on them while they were talking. Good thing he hadn't acted on his idea of rubbing off on Mikhail despite the fact that his mate smelled amazingly good.

"But I'm the captain," Jin protested. "Your father would be justified in punishing me for not training my men correctly."

The thought of the king's displeasure put a chill down his spine. He'd fought hard for his position as Captain of the Guard. However, he deserved anything the royal wanted to mete out. He had allowed Eliza to be kidnapped—he was ultimately responsible. She could've been killed or, worse, used as a baby incubator by ruthless sirens.

Mikhail must have picked up on his concerns. "I won't let anything happen to you," he vowed.

A glow of warmth went through Jin, and for once, it had nothing to do with the fire banked in his gut.

Eliza gave an inelegant snort. "I don't know that there is much a siren-vamp can do to my father."

Mikhail grinned, not his usual pleasant expression but the smile of a hunter ready to take out his prey. "Never underestimate other paras, Princess—we are more resourceful than you know."

Jin sensed Eliza winding herself up to ask questions. "Why don't you go with Sam and see if there are any snacks in the little shop? I'll wait for you out here." He gave Eliza a little push toward the other pair. With one last look at Mikhail, she rushed to comply.

"Feel better for scaring a little girl?" Jin folded his arms in front of him and glared at his mate.

Mikhail shrugged, not appearing the least bit repentant. "She needs to learn not to underestimate others. One day, if she is queen, she could make a big mistake if she thinks other paranormals can't take on a dragon. One on one, she might be right, but sirens and vamps rarely attack head on. Deception can topple a kingdom faster than might."

"True." Jin wanted to hold onto his annoyance, but Mikhail had a good point. Eliza could run into trouble if she discounted other paranormals, and that could end in her death. She had enough enemies already. Particularly if it was true that someone, another dragon, had sold her to get her out of the line for succession.

"I don't know if I can live in a dragon mound." Anxiety clouded Mikhail's eyes.

"Try, my mate. Only a few dragons can survive in the city, and I don't know if I am one of them."

There again, Jin thought he might have no choice. If the king kicked him out, he might not have a chance to decide if he wanted to stay or not. He might be exiled.

"I'll try. Maybe we can do a fifty-fifty relationship. Half of the time in your mountain and half out." Mikhail's eyes widened as if he'd only just realized what he had said. He'd virtually admitted that he was considering being with Jin permanently. Jin wished he could push the advantage and have Mikhail commit to him, but now was not the time. For some reason he felt edgy and he shrugged his shoulders to release some of the tension.

Jin kissed Mikhail's forehead. "Let's wait and see."

No reason to commit to anything if he didn't know the situation back home. The tension became a warning tingle and suddenly every nerve was alive to the possibility of a threat.

"They are near."

The whispers of displaced air had Jin grabbing Mikhail and dragging him to the ground. He shifted into his dragon form just as flames poured from the sky and danced across his back. Fire spilled harmlessly off his scales.

"Run!" he telepathically screamed at Mikhail.

Mikhail ran toward the building. Jin took to the sky. Shrieking his displeasure at the attack, he rushed at a dragon circling them. The large beast was sapphire blue, and Jin immediately knew who he was facing. He recognized the beast as his younger brother, Nillon. What was happening? Why was Nillon trying to kill them? Was the princess in danger? Jin would die before he let his brother hurt Eliza.

Whipping around the blue dragon, he slashed a claw across Nillon's back. The blue dragon tumbled to earth with a roar. Immediately, Nillon was back on all four legs and leaping straight back into Jin. They tumbled as they fought, and, after a brief tussle, Jin had his brother pinned. He looked directly into sapphire eyes and incredible hurt raced through him. He had thought his brother an idiot, but he had never thought he was one of the bad guys. What motivation could his brother have in coming to attack their future ruler?

"Why do you attack the princess?" Jin demanded. Nillon used his body weight to spin their positions until he had the upper hand.

"I'm not here for her. I'm here for you!" Nillon's words shouted into Jin's head.

Jin struggled under his brother, and with a frustrated roar, he pushed him away. Nillon stumbled back and scraped claws along Sam's car to steady himself.

"Why?" Jin asked.

Nillon took advantage of his momentary hesitation and swiped a claw to split Jin's scales on his chest. Jin reared back and avoided most of the slice, then, in a final push, he pinned Nillon to the ground, using his tail as leverage to keep him still.

"Tell me what you mean," Jin demanded. He was so intent on getting Nillon to talk that he almost missed the golden dragon swooping down. It was only the flash of scales in the car mirror that caught his eye. Flipping around, he ducked in time for the newcomer to slam into Nillon.

With a loud trumpet of anger, the new arrival toppled to the ground next to Nillon.

Jin landed beside them. The golden dragon shifted. Jin recognized him as Smoke, a distant relation of his and a strong warrior. Smoke wasn't his real name, but Jin couldn't remember the golden dragon's birth name at the moment. Smoke looked pointedly at Nillon, who tilted his head, then shifted. Jin did the same.

"Will one of you tell me what is going on?" Jin asked immediately.

"The king demanded your death for kidnapping the princess," Nillon growled. He stepped forward, but Smoke held his arm.

"And I am here to help him kill you," Smoke said. "Do you have any last words?"

Smoke was part of the death squad as well?

"Kidnapping? I'm bringing her back!" Confusion swirled through Jin's head. "Who said I kidnapped her?" Both of these dragons served under him. He had thought he had their absolute trust and loyalty—it devastated him to hear that they believed he would hurt Eliza and that they had willingly undertaken the task of hunting him down.

Nillon's narrow-eyed glare had Jin grinding his teeth. It was Smoke who answered. "Meel," he said.

Jin's mouth dropped open. Meel? The king's brother? Meel had told the king that Jin had kidnapped Eliza?

"You're right," Jin said. Smoke stepped forward with a snarl. Jin held up a hand to forestall any more words. He had to explain this to the dragons. "She *was* kidnapped. Someone took her, but it wasn't me. I heard her song, found her, and I'm bringing her home."

"With humans?" Smoke folded his arms and his expression was troubled. "We were told you were using humans to keep Eliza from us," he said.

Jin held up a hand to stop whatever Smoke was going to say next. "Sam Enderson is a renowned investigator," Jin exaggerated. He had no idea how good Sam was, but Eliza was convinced that Sam was good. "He is coming with us to investigate Eliza's kidnapping. The sirens were using a dragon heart to locate her."

"But they're all under lock and key," Nillon said urgently.

Jin shrugged. "Someone must have opened up the vault and stolen one."

The shock on both the dragon shifters' faces assured Jin that they were as surprised as him.

Nillon stepped forward. "We will accompany you. If what you say is true—"

"Of course it's true," Jin said. "Why would I lie?"

"Let me finish, Captain," Nillon said. "If we believe you, then there is the small matter of the king's intel being faulty."

Smoke nodded his agreement. "Which is what I was telling Nillon last night," he said.

"You never said anything," Nillon replied quickly.

"I said I didn't believe Jin would be a traitor," Smoke said, scowling.

"Exactly what I said as well." Nillon bared his teeth and puffed a small amount of smoke.

Jin watched the exchange with disbelief. They didn't have time to argue here. When the King, or Meel, or whoever was behind this realized that the first wave of dragons hadn't returned with Jin's body—or Eliza's—they would surely send more.

He interrupted the verbal sparring. "This brings us to the question of who is really behind this."

"Someone who is trying to get the princess permanently removed from the line of succession by killing her." Nillon shook his head sadly.

"Whoever it is has to die," Smoke said.

"We shouldn't judge anyone until we have all the facts,"

Jin hastened to point out. "We need to wait to see what Meel's intelligence was. And what the king has to say about any evidence of my guilt."

The fact that the king had been so quick to listen to unfounded allegations—to judge Jin and send him to his death—sent a chill through his bones. He'd served the king for centuries and the royal had tossed him away without thought. Blood was always worth more than loyal service it appeared.

"Is there a problem here?" Sam's hard tone had the three dragons turning to face the newcomer.

Sam stood between the two vamps with Eliza hovering near Mikhail. Jin appreciated the comforting hand Mikhail had placed on Eliza's shoulder as if he could sense her distress.

The two dragon shifters bowed to their princess.

"Nillon. Smoke. What are you doing here?" Eliza asked, confused. Then her face brightened. "Did Daddy send you for me?"

The two dragons exchanged an uncomfortable look. Jin remembered what they'd said.

"They were worried I'd kidnapped you," Jin intercepted. If one of these men were going to take his position as captain, with the responsibility of guarding the princess, he didn't want to cause her to distrust them.

"Jin saved me! The sirens were coming to take me again. Sam and his friends rescued me the first time, but Jin and Mikhail protected me from them the second time." Her words tumbled out in a long sentence, and then she looked to Jin for what to say next.

Jin recalled Eliza neatly saving herself, but he didn't interrupt. If the princess wanted to interpret his appearance as a rescue, he wouldn't deny her. After all, he needed all the support he could get.

"Then the king has been misinformed," Smoke said smoothly. He slid an interested gaze across Sam. "Who is this?"

Bob bared his fangs at the dragon. "My mate."

Smoke growled. Bob snarled back.

Sam rolled his eyes at the paranormal stand-off. "I'm Sam Enderson. These are my friends, Bob and Mikhail."

Jin waited for Bob's reaction. If Bob were a dragon, Sam would've been incinerated on the spot. "I'm more than a friend," Bob corrected sternly.

Sam sighed. "Fine. This is my mate, the love of my life, the one I can't live without," Sam said in a bored tone. "Better?"

"Much." Bob grinned, showing off his fangs at the other dragons. "So keep your hands to yourself, Scales."

Smoke ignored Bob, but instead of a lustful leer, he was now observing Sam with a puzzled expression on his face. "What are you?" he asked Sam.

"Human." Sam's tone indicated that further conversation was not welcome.

Jin watched in amusement as both of the vampires shook their head at Smoke, subtly showing that Smoke should stop asking questions.

"All right then." Smoke turned and exchanged looks with Jin. Jin knew that wasn't the end of the discussion over Sam's heritage. Smoke had always been one of the most observant of his lieutenants and Jin agreed with Smoke's confusion. There was definitely something strange about the *supposed* human. He just couldn't put his finger on it.

"We can fly above the car and watch out for others the

king might have sent," Nillon offered. His interruption stopped all the posturing and questions.

"Thank you. I appreciate your help." Jin hoped the two knew how grateful he truly was. If they'd chosen not to believe him, they could've killed him with the king's blessing. Smoke was clearly there because he hadn't automatically believed their king's intel. To question the king? That was heresy. Things must've become worse at the mountain since Jin had been there, and he'd only been gone two months.

After Eliza's disappearance, he'd left the king's palace cave to investigate where she might be. When he'd left, there had already been signs of weakness and corruption in the king's extended family. Apparently, Meel had been busy poisoning his brother against Jin. The question was why?

"I am sorry, brother," Nillon said. His cheeks glowed bright with shame. "I shouldn't have blindly followed orders. I knew in my heart that you would never betray the princess. They confused me with promises that I would have your place when you died." He hesitated. Jin touched him on the arm but said nothing. "Greed and envy were my downfall."

Smoke muttered something under his breath, which Jin didn't hear but which Nillon clearly did. He glared at Smoke, but Smoke ignored him. "I would've been a good guard for the princess," he added.

"You might still get your chance," Jin said dryly. "I knew something was wrong when I left, but I didn't realize everything was so bad. My faith in the king's support is a bit shaken."

What kind of man orders a person killed without hearing their side of the story?

"He's changed much in the past few months. The loss of his daughter broke him," Smoke explained. "We all thought she was dead. We couldn't hear her song anymore. I wonder, even with Eliza's return, if he will ever be the same."

"We must make haste and see if we can pull our ruler from his sorrow," Jin said. Silently, he wondered if he could ever trust the king again or if the kingdom could be saved. He hoped he wouldn't have to become a city dragon after all.

Chapter Five

THEY COMPLETED THE REST OF THE JOURNEY IN SILENCE. Mikhail missed having Jin in the car, but the dragon shifter had decided to fly above the car on point and have Nillon sit in the car. Every so often, the sun hit Jin at the right angle and revealed the beautiful shadow of his dragon form. Flying beside Jin was Smoke, the gorgeous gold dragon who had really upset Bob.

In fact, Bob becoming all possessive was probably why Sam stayed quiet. Once in a while, he would glance sideways at Bob. Mikhail waited for the heated debate over Bob's nature, but it never came. Although they bickered like kids, at times the connection between Bob and his mate was absolute. Sam had come around to the whole situation quite well for a human… or at least a kind of human. Eliza slept, curled into Nillon's side. Nillon's rhythmic snoring was the only noise in the car, and Mikhail wished Sam would turn on some music. He was irritable, and being forced into the back of the car with two dragons, who, even in human form, gave off a lot of body heat, had him feeling closed in and crushed. Not to mention the acrid smell of the smoke Nillon exhaled with each snore.

He idly considered whether Jin would give him a ride on his back.

"No, mate," Jin said in his head with a laugh.

"You can hear me even up there?" Mikhail asked curiously. He leaned over Nillon's body and peered out of the window. Jin swooped down from up high and hovered close to the car, a shimmering scarlet against the blue sky with its scattered white clouds.

"I can hear everything. Why do you think I keep casting shadows over you?"

"What can you see from up there?"

"My home. The mountain peaks that defy the ground and rise high above the clouds."

"Sounds better than listening to Nillon snoring."

Smoke joined Jin as they slowly tracked with the car, flanking the vehicle. The strange procession began to climb up into the mountains.

"They do that for our protection," Nillon said softly.

Mikhail turned to face Jin's brother. His opinion of Nillon, quite apart from the irritating snoring, wasn't good. He wasn't sure if it was the mate bond or something else, but Nillon's belief that Jin was a traitor grated at Mikhail. He still didn't trust the third dragon in this little group. His opinion didn't change when Nillon awoke either.

"So why aren't you out there?" Mikhail asked irritably.

"Someone needs to stay close to the princess," Nillon said. He used a tone that sounded like Nillon thought Mikhail was an idiot for asking.

"So why not Jin? He's the one who found her."

"Jin is a great warrior. Maybe the greatest dragon guard

the mountains have ever known, but I have my place here as the last defense. If something happened, I would take the princess and fly."

Nillon spoke firmly, and Mikhail felt pride race through him that Jin, his dragon, was respected. Then it hit him what Nillon had said.

"You say all that, but you still doubted him?" Mikhail scolded.

"When a dragon is as old as Jin and hasn't mated, they often become unstable." Nillon shrugged. "I was handed evidence and given my orders. That is my role."

Mikhail kept to himself what an idiot he thought Nillon was. He couldn't help thinking it, though, and he heard Jin chuckle in his thoughts.

"Up ahead is the gate." Nillon interrupted Mikhail listening to the beautiful tones of his dragon's laughter. "Once past there, we can feel safe."

Mikhail didn't say what he thought—that he didn't think traveling into a dragon's clutch was safe, especially for dragons who didn't have the support of the king.

There was no guard at the gate, no one stopped their journey, and finally they pulled up outside a huge sprawling wall that, on the end nearest to them, gave the illusion of disappearing inside the mountain. There was a small group of people waiting for them.

"There's His Majesty," Nillon said proudly. Eliza jumped out of the car as soon as the vehicle stopped. She ran straight into the arms of an older man with startlingly white hair. He scooped her up in his arms and held her tight for a long time. Mikhail climbed out and stood with Bob and Sam. Jin landed next to them and shifted in an instant. The flowing red shirt he now wore pressed to his skin in the breeze; he was as magnificent in human form as he was as a dragon. Smoke landed, shifted, and flanked the other side of them.

A man detached himself from the small welcoming party and immediately rushed to Jin before pulling him into a close hug. Mikhail sensed Jin tense and heard the curse word in his thoughts.

"Ryujin, we thought you were dead," the stranger said. Mikhail didn't have to be empathic to hear the falseness in that welcome. Also, what was going on with the new guy plastering himself all over Jin? Mikhail did not like that one bit. Possessively, he moved close to Jin and threaded his fingers through the dragon's. Jin didn't argue. If anything, he gripped harder.

"I'd like to present Mikhail, my mate," Jin said firmly. "Mikhail, this is Meel, brother to the king and Eliza's uncle."

"Your mate?" Meel looked positively sick for an instant, but the expression soon cleared. "What is he?" Meel looked Mikhail up and down and even went so far as to sniff the air. "A vampire? A siren? Both? Neither?"

"My mother was a siren queen, my father a vampire." Mikhail spoke firmly and waited for further disgust. There was none. Seemed Mikhail wasn't important in Meel's eyes because he turned his attention back to Jin.

"Does he know and accept the ritual? Have you been with him?" Meel asked.

"I will explain the ritual to him later, and no, we have not fully mated."

Relief sparked in Meel's eyes. "Then there is still time to keep the purity intact," he muttered. Everyone heard him, but Mikhail didn't have time to say anything. Quickly changing the subject, Meel herded the visitors toward the king, who was still cuddling Eliza close and laughing as she spoke in his ear.

"Your Highness," Jin said formally. He dropped Mikhail's hand, fell to one knee and bowed his head. Smoke and Nillon did the same. Mikhail bowed his head and watched Bob and Sam copy him with the sign of respect.

"These are the ones who saved me the first time," Eliza said. "Sam and Bob and Mikhail and their friends. They got me from the warehouse where the humans and sirens had me and lots of other girls. Then, when the sirens used the dragon heart to find me, Mikhail put himself between me and them. Jin came through and Mikhail pushed me out of Jin's way 'cause he thought Jin was going to hurt me." Mikhail smiled at the dragon princess's enthusiasm and her run-on sentences.

"You are welcome to stay here under my protection," the king offered. He looked at Meel. "Please take our guests to find rooms, Meel. Jin, I need to speak to you in my chambers."

"It will be fine." Mikhail heard Jin's thoughts. Jin, the king, and Eliza left in one direction as Meel guided them in another.

They traveled down wide and high-vaulted corridors until they reached a series of large wooden doors. Worryingly, the room Mikhail was given had a door with burn marks on it. Sam and Bob hovered outside their room, and as soon as the three were left alone, they all went into Mikhail's room. Bob spoke first.

"I don't like Meel," he said firmly.

Mikhail was quick to agree. "I don't trust him," he said.

Bob pulled Sam close. "I don't like Smoke either."

Sam cradled Bob's face and kissed him passionately and deeply. "Shhh," he said when he pulled back. "Stop with the jealousy. It's distracting in my head." Sam tapped his left temple with a finger.

"I can't help it," Bob offered. "I love you, and when he touched you—"

Sam nearly climbed Bob in his enthusiasm to prove that there was no one else for him but Bob. "I love you—"

"Stop!" Mikhail ordered. "Do that love stuff later. Right now, we have a case."

Sam appeared to snap out of the *I love you*'s pretty quickly and stepped away from Bob. "Agreed," he said firmly. Cracking his neck, he placed his hands on his hips. "So this is what we know. A dragon opened a vault here, stole a dragon's heart, gave it to the sirens, and then used it to make a portal into my bathroom on the second floor. Two sirens came through the portal, Jin arrived and rescued Eliza, reducing one siren to a crispy critter. Meel supposedly had evidence that Jin was going to kill Eliza if the sirens failed, which we know isn't true. Did I miss anything?"

Mikhail shook his head. He could have added the whole dragon mate ritual thing to the list but kept it in his head. That was his and Jin's issue and had nothing to do with the case.

Sam continued, "What I don't understand is how easily Meel managed to convince the king that Jin was guilty of kidnapping Eliza. What did Meel have in the way of evidence?"

"There is no evidence."

Jin's gravelly voice startled Mikhail. He spun on his heel to face Jin.

Sam frowned. "What do you mean?"

"The king and I have just spoken. He wasn't shown any physical evidence. He doesn't remember much about what was happening because he was grieving. He thought Eliza was dead. He left the decisions and the ruling of the kingdom to Meel." Jin slumped down on the huge bed in the middle of

Mikhail's room. "Meel has to be the person we look to for betrayal."

"I'm sorry, Jin," Mikhail offered gently.

Sam stepped forward. "Can I see the vault?"

Jin shook his head. "The vault is in the temple itself. Only dragonkin can enter and only after the death of another dragon when a new spirit is deposited."

"So we can rule out sirens getting in here and helping themselves," Bob summarized.

"It was definitely a dragon or…" Jin paused. "There is another way someone could get in. But because we keep ourselves so insular, it doesn't happen often."

"Tell us."

"A non-dragonkin could enter the vault during a mating ceremony. As part of the ritual, the vault is opened for the union to be blessed by the old spirits inside."

Bob looked impressed. "So then we could get inside when you and Mikhail mate properly—"

"If we mate," Mikhail snapped. He wished people wouldn't assume this was a done deal. Then he realized what he had done.

Silence fell in the group before Sam edged Bob out of the door, saying they would see Mikhail and Jin later.

Mikhail exhaled and turned to face his dragon.

"I will not make you mine if you don't want to be," Jin offered gently. His big silver eyes were wet with emotion. Could dragons cry?

"Jin, I'm sorry." Mikhail stepped forward and placed a hand on Jin's chest. He felt it's rise and fall as Jin breathed, and he matched his own breathing to that of the dragon. "I feel like I'm being backed into a corner, and it isn't a nice feeling. Like it's a done deal after two days."

"I don't mean to," Jin said. He placed a hand over Mikhail's. "I can't help what I want."

"Can I tell you something that could help you understand why my head rules my heart?" Mikhail asked. Jin nodded. "Until I was ten, I lived as a siren prince in the sea and I was destined to rule my own pod. My mother and father doted on me. I was blessed. Then, when puberty hit, my vampiric nature became stronger and suddenly I was no longer a prince, but an unwanted bastard child from a woman who had cheated on her husband. I was pushed out, beaten, exiled— they killed my mom. I had no one. I wasn't a siren. I wasn't a vampire. I was a crossbreed with no family... until I met Bob. He's my family now, for what it's worth."

"I am sorry, my mate," Jin said quietly.

"I choose my own path, I am stubborn and opinionated, and I will argue with you every day, but I'm not rejecting you."

"I like you just as you are," Jin reassured him.

Mikhail felt his heart constrict. "It's all so quick; I've seen the instant connection with others. I just never imagined it would happen to me that way because of my mixed blood, or that my fated mate would be a dragon. I want you. I want you so much it burns me inside and I've never felt that way before."

"It sounds like you have a but?" Jin prompted.

"Is that what being your mate means? Like I want to lie next to you and never leave?"

Jin pulled him close and the scent of *his* dragon filled Mikhail's senses—fire and fall and spice. His cock filled, and he wanted more. He wanted to kiss Jin and love him, and he knew he had to accept that he was worthy of being a dragon's mate.

"You will always be worthy." Jin's voice was gentle, and he cradled Mikhail's head against his chest.

"I guess you'd better explain about this ritual," Mikhail murmured against the soft textured shirt.

Jin tightened his hold.

"I don't want you to panic, my mate, but it starts with fire."

Chapter Six

"Fire?" Mikhail had never been a fan of flames, at least not until he'd met a certain dragon shifter who had turned him inside out. Sirens didn't tend to do well with anything that would dry out their skin.

Jin smiled. "Not all flames are the same. Dragons have several different kinds of flames. Some have heat. Some don't."

"And the mating flame?" Mikhail asked, worried. He didn't believe Jin would hurt him intentionally, but what didn't hurt a dragon might not be as friendly toward a vampire-siren crossbreed.

"We'll worry about that when you're ready. I don't want you to get worked up about the ceremony. No mate picked by the gods has ever been burned to death during the mating ritual," Jin reassured.

Mikhail returned Jin's smile with a hesitant one of his own. Did he really want this? Did he want to be bonded to a dragon shifter? Looking into Jin's eyes, he realized he didn't really have a choice. He could feel the connection twisting between them. If he rejected Jin, he would always be alone.

"Okay, once we get this whole kidnapped princess thing settled, we need to talk. I have to say I am shocked about your king demanding your death without even finding out the facts. I don't see how worrying about his daughter would allow him to blindly order a loyal soldier's death. I don't know if I can respect him as a leader." Mikhail meant every word. He wasn't a forgive-and-forget type of person, especially when one careless mistake would've meant the death of his mate.

Damn, now even he was calling Jin his mate inside his head.

Jin grinned.

Mikhail rolled his eyes at the dragon shifter's excitement. "Shut up. Let's go get Sam and Bob. We can start interviewing dragons. If what we heard about Meel influencing the king is true, we need to corner him and find out if he's the one who sold out the princess. Once we gather proof, we can give it to your king and keep her safe."

Jin scowled. "He will be your king too."

"Maybe. I'm not so quick to swear my allegiance. I want to see what he has to say for himself."

"You can't interrogate a king!" Jin protested.

Memories of his treatment from the hands of his own king crowded Mikhail's mind. "Keeping you safe is my priority."

Dragons might be physically stronger than a siren or a vampire, but Mikhail hadn't survived as long as he had by being all sunshine and rainbows. He'd turn the shifters inside out with a siren song if necessary. The fuckers didn't know who they were messing with.

Mikhail sent out a psychic call to locate Bob until it bounced back at him. He kept the thought deep inside so it wouldn't spill over to Jin, but he privately thought the dragon nest was more like a pit of vipers. Hopefully, they wouldn't have to interact with the others very often.

"Hey, guys," Sam greeted them with a wide smile. His eyes were a bit bright and his lips puffy so Mikhail had a good idea how the two men had spent their time. Bob's smug expression supported his suspicions that they had been kissing.

"We need to start questioning dragons," Mikhail said by way of hello.

Bob nodded, his gaze darting quickly to Jin as if judging how the shifter took Mikhail's statement.

"I agree," Jin confirmed.

"We talked to a couple of them and they all said Smoke was the one who told them Jin had turned on the king, but that it came from Meel," Bob confessed.

Apparently, his friends had been busy in more than one way since they had parted.

"Who did you talk to?" Jin asked.

Bob rattled off several names, none of which Mikhail recognized. He could tell from Jin's expression that he did.

"All of them said it was Smoke? Maybe he was just following Meel's orders..." Jin began pacing the room.

"There was one other thing..." Sam said uncertainly. He looked uncomfortable.

"What?" Jin snapped. He came and stood in front of Sam.

"Slaiths? I think that was his name—he speaks with a slurred voice"—Jin nodded to indicate that the name was right—"He said it was odd. Those were the words he used. Smoke told Slaiths that Nillon and he were tracking you down to take you out."

Mikhail watched Jin's expression as he waited for the punch line. "There's nothing odd about that," Jin said gently. "Dragons know other dragons' business."

"It's odd because Slaiths then went on to say that he saw Meel in the corridor soon after. When they passed pleasantries—his words, not mine—Meel seemed surprised, even shocked, that Smoke and Nillon had left. Not just shocked, but furious. Then he left immediately and said something about seeing the king. We also have a... Abberin" —Sam checked his notes—"who says he witnessed Meel entering the king's room and looking very nervous."

Jin exhaled noisily and Sam waved a hand to clear the puff of smoke. He continued, "So if Meel didn't know about Smoke and Nillon, then Smoke was lying to Slaiths." For a short while Jin appeared to be fighting the urge to dragon out —his hands clenched into fists at his sides and his skin changed color. Finally, he had himself under control and he started for the door.

Mikhail purposely stood in his path to block his way. "Relax, Jin, we'll get to the bottom of this."

"I never trusted Meel, but I loved Smoke like a brother." Jin's broken expression squeezed Mikhail's heart.

"I know, mate." Mikhail wrapped his arms around the dragon shifter. "I'm so sorry."

Mikhail remembered vividly how betrayal twisted a person's gut and tore them to shreds. Sirens he'd thought were his friends had beaten or turned their backs on him when his lineage came to light. Nothing cut deeper than a knife plunged into your back.

"He might be after your job," Sam offered. "A couple of dragons we spoke to mentioned Smoke's ambition. He can't go any higher if you are standing in his way."

"I would've stepped aside," Jin replied. "I only took the position because no one else stepped up and challenged me during the trials. If Smoke had asked, I would've let him battle me for the job."

"I don't think he wants to become Captain by following rules," Mikhail said. His instinctive dislike of Smoke hadn't been a fluke. The guy had apparently been a slimeball anyway.

"Let's go talk to Meel and find out what he has to say." Mikhail's stomach twisted into knots as he remembered the dragon shifter's attention to Jin. "Have you and Meel ever been together?" Mikhail asked. He recalled the way Meel had dismissed Mikhail as unworthy.

Jin nodded. "Of course. The number of gay dragons isn't high. We experimented together when we were younger, but we sort of drifted apart over time. We were never the great love story. He wasn't the most faithful and he would lie, even then, to get himself out of situations."

"Which is why you immediately believed Smoke when he said Meel was guilty," Mikhail said.

"Yeah, Meel has always been a bit on the sneaky side. Everyone knows he wants to be king. It wasn't such a leap to think he'd get rid of the king's captain to weaken the holder of the throne."

"Smoke was counting on no one asking questions," Sam said. "If you were dead and the princess lost to the sirens, there wouldn't be anyone to question Meel's supposed orders through the king. Except Meel himself. It's rather clever when you think about it."

"Clever!" Jin growled. "I almost died." His eyes glowed with fire for a brief moment, replacing his silvery orbs with pure flame.

"Easy, love—Sam is just thinking out loud." Mikhail flashed Sam a warning look that the human responded to with a shrug.

Bob pushed Sam a little behind him, protecting his mate from the dragon's wrath. "Let's focus on Smoke and find out what really happened. Do you know where to find him? We tried to track him down, but no one knows where he is."

"We should check his chambers," Jin suggested. He headed down the corridor and the others followed the short distance to a large oak door.

Mikhail nearly walked into his back when Jin came to a dead stop.

"What's wrong?"

"There is a spell on Smoke's door, stopping us from getting inside," Jin said with a shudder. He wrapped his hands around his middle. "It's cold magic. We'll need a wizard to get inside."

"Can you see through it? Is Smoke inside?"

Jin tilted his head and closed his eyes. "I can see books open on the desk, his bed, unmade, an open bag on the bed. Looks as if he was leaving in a hurry."

"After we interviewed him maybe?" Sam said.

"He's thrown magic up as a barrier."

"We need to find Meel," Mikhail stated simply. "Warn him and the king about what is happening here."

"Maybe Meel is with the king," Jin said.

MIKHAIL NODDED. That made sense. The four of them headed to the royal chambers, only to be stopped by guards at the entrance.

"We've come to talk to the king," Sam told the largest of the guards.

Mikhail wondered briefly if Sam simply had no fear. For someone who proclaimed not to like paras, it certainly wasn't owing to a fear of them. Sam never backed down from anyone. Mikhail didn't know if it was owing to bravery or if Sam just didn't have any sense of self-preservation.

"The king cannot see you right now," the guard said. The dragon shifter stepped forward to block Sam's way.

"We believe the king's brother is inside with him and we have questions for him," Sam said.

Mikhail saw Bob step up to Sam's side, but he didn't interfere. "Meel isn't here. He went to talk to Smoke," the guard offered.

"Where?" Sam asked.

Mikhail knew the human had the same sense of urgency as the rest of them over finding Meel as quickly as possible. Meel being with Smoke couldn't be a good thing. If what they suspected was true, that Meel was innocent in this, then the king's brother could be in trouble.

"I heard Smoke say they should talk and that he wanted Meel to accompany him to the entrance to the southern caverns. Something about locating a traitor now that you have returned." The guard looked nervous. After all, he was accusing his captain. "Smoke was most insistent, and Meel didn't argue," the guard added.

"Let's go!" Jin said. "Follow me."

The rest of them dutifully followed.

Jin picked up speed as they rushed down the hall, dodging to avoid others. Time was of the essence. They had to get to Meel before Smoke did something.

Mikhail didn't know how the dragons could determine the direction of their chambers. Underground, with all the twists and turns, Mikhail quickly lost his sense of where they were.

Turning the corner, they caught sight of Smoke and Meel. Smoke had Meel pushed up against the wall and Meel looked terrified.

"Hey!" Jin shouted.

Smoke turned his head. Catching sight of the group, he

flashed them a small, victorious smile. He threw something on the ground. Seconds later, green smoke filled the hall.

"No!" Jin shouted.

Mikhail blinked rapidly as his eyes watered from the acrid smoke. "That burns!" he shouted.

Jin shot a burst of flame at the smoke, burning away the green cloud hanging in the air. Mikhail turned to his friends to find Bob on the ground and Sam standing over him. Sam's hands glowed a blinding white and the air around him crackled with energy. No sign of green smoke dared to hover near the pair. Sam was looking down at his hands with shock.

"Are you sure he's human?" Jin asked in a low voice.

"That's what he says," Mikhail replied. He wondered if Sam was as tired of answering that question as Mikhail.

Several minutes later, after all the smoke had cleared from the hall, they found that both Smoke and Meel had disappeared.

"What was that?" Sam asked. His hands stopped glowing as he leaned down to help Bob to his feet. Bob's skin, pale even for a vampire, had a greenish hue not unlike the smoke that had magically cleared out of the hall.

"It's a smoke bomb. They are rare and difficult to make, but Smoke is an expert. It's one of the reasons for his nickname. There is no way to instantly track the destination. He'll have gone into the mountains." Devastation was written across the dragon shifter's face. "How could I not have seen Smoke was behind all of this?"

Mikhail couldn't let Jin blame himself. "You were too upset with Eliza missing. You didn't suspect she was a victim of one of your own. After all, you didn't even know until recently that she'd been kidnapped."

Jin nodded. "True. I had hoped she'd run away or gotten lost or anything other than being betrayed by one of her people. We'll need to begin a tracking spell, but it takes a while to locate any dragon who used smoke magic to disappear. We need to talk to the king and try to figure out where Smoke might have taken Meel. He is the only one powerful enough to create a location spell."

"We need some sleep," Sam said. "We've traveled all day. Let's talk to the king now and tomorrow we can look into possibly tracking Smoke. Get this spell you talk about. Meanwhile, Bob and I need to figure out Smoke's habits and friends. Then we can back up the spells with detective work. Someone must've suspected him of something along the way. No one is that perfect. Everyone slips up somewhere."

"True," Mikhail agreed. There wasn't such a thing as the perfect crime. "Let's go back to the king, then talk to his guard friends."

With that plan in place, they went back the way they had come.

"I CAN'T BELIEVE the king didn't suspect anything," Mikhail said. He knew his voice had a whine to it, but frankly the king had to be the most clueless ruler he'd ever met. The king had not only told Jin to take care of the problem, but had threatened to take away his title as Captain of the Guards if he didn't buckle down and deal with Smoke. At least he had set the location spell to start.

"He's trying to motivate me," Jin said as if the king's tactics made sense and weren't the wild ravings of a dragon shifter about to get his ass kicked.

"He's going to motivate me to execute a king," Mikhail growled.

Jin laughed even as he gently scolded, "You shouldn't threaten a monarch."

"I haven't threatened him yet. Besides, I don't threaten. I promise and follow through. I hate it when stupid people are in charge."

"He's not stupid," Jin said. A sigh escaped him as he strove to explain about his kind. "He's really, really old, and I think sometimes all his past memories take over his mind and he has difficulty remembering things like who is on his side."

"He's senile?" Mikhail asked. It was starting to make sense. If the king's sanity was beginning to fray from his long life, then he might not be able to determine the difference between who would support him and who might stab him in the chest.·

Jin shuffled his feet. "I wouldn't say he was crazy, but he definitely doesn't have the same edge he used to."

Mikhail thought Jin was just splitting hairs.

"So to prevent Monarch McCrazy from firing you, we need to find his brother, pursue Smoke to wherever he went, and bring Meel back. Did he at least assign guards to help you?"

"No. He said I caused this problem by not catching Smoke sooner."

Mikhail gritted his teeth and held back the words threatening to spew like verbal acid across the room.

Jin shook his head. "Like Sam said, let's get a good night's sleep."

Mikhail doubted either of them would sleep much, but he stripped down and climbed onto the bed. "Do I get a teddy bear to sleep with?" he asked, flashing a sultry look to Jin through his lashes.

Jin grinned. "Honey, naked like that, I'll give you anything you want."

Licking his lips, Mikhail knew just how to burn away the frustration and bits of rage coursing through his body. He'd get even with the king for putting his mate into this much danger if it was the last thing he ever did. Until then, he had much better things to do to occupy his time.

Chapter Seven

"THE FIRST TIME HAS TO BE ON THE HALLOWED GROUND OF A dragon's chamber," Jin said softly.

"Our first time?" Mikhail glanced around Jin's room. The ceilings were tall, the space large, and a huge sliding window faced out over a sharp and jagged peak of the mountain. There was nothing in the place to indicate that it was hallowed ground. But, as Jin clearly wanted to take things further between them, he must have brought them back to the room for a reason.

"When a dragon comes of age, they are given a special chamber inside the castle walls that is blessed by the ancient families."

Mikhail felt the weight of expectation on him. "And you said no *mate* picked by the gods has ever been burned to death during the rituals. Including this one—our first time?" Mikhail wanted to be sure.

"Yes."

"How can you be sure?"

Jin stepped closer and held out his right hand. "Watch."

Mikhail looked down at Jin's palm and watched curiously

as a tiny thread of sparkling silver and white light formed in the middle. It grew in size, twisting and spinning until it was as tall as the room and disappeared up into the darkness of the ceiling space where it cast an eerie glow. The stream of light was utterly beautiful, and when he followed it down to glance at Jin, he saw a similar color in the dragon's eyes. Not fire. White.

"What is that?" Mikhail asked.

Jin smiled, then reached up with his other hand and summoned the other end of the stream of silvery white. The length of it, a living thing, wrapped around Jin, his back, his chest, then looped out and settled around Mikhail.

Mikhail gasped and tensed as the white touched him. At first, the touch was gentle, then it became more insistent and tugged him closer to Jin until they were as close as they could be without bodily contact.

"The mating bond," Jin said gently. "I can only create this with my true fated mate. Bob and Sam have this between them."

Mikhail frowned. "They do? I haven't seen it."

"Only dragons and their mates can see it."

"It's beautiful." Mikhail reached up and touched the light with his fingers. A snap of electricity passed through him, chased quickly by immediate lust and need. The strings of color flickered and pressed him closer to Jin.

Jin tilted his head and kissed Mikhail. The dragon was hard and demanding and needy. Mikhail reached up and buried his hands into Jin's hair, it's softness wrapping around his fingers as the light had just done. He was aroused to the point of losing control right here and now, but the insistent push of Jin's cock against his was not enough. He wanted more. He had the sensation of movement, then he was lying on the wide, solid bed. Had Jin carried him? He didn't care.

All he knew was that Jin covered him and kissed him and pushed him higher.

Jin was warm and his eyes still glowed with silver pinpricks in the white. They were stunning, filled with light and entirely focused on Mikhail as Jin kissed a path from Mikhail's lips to his throat.

"I'm not burning," Mikhail breathed. He wanted more—Jin in him—and he wanted it now. "It's okay." Everything was a dream of raw, passionate lust and want.

"My mate…" Jin whispered into Mikhail's ear. He caressed Mikhail from shoulder to chest and focused intently on Mikhail's left nipple, kissing, tugging, and with every movement, talking softly in a language Mikhail didn't know. Mikhail realized he was lying there and not participating, and while that was as close to any kind of heaven he'd ever experienced, he really wanted to get his hands on Jin. He closed his arms around the sexy dragon and ran his hands down to Jin's ass, cupping and kneading and arching to kiss Jin some more.

He settled into a rhythm of press and release, finding the right groove between Jin's hip and groin and losing himself to the sensations that rushed through him. His cock sliding against Jin's was perfect, and he'd never felt a need like this ever before.

"Only me," Jin whispered. Mikhail didn't have to ask what he meant. He knew. Inside, he was absolutely certain there would be no other man for Mikhail. Jin was his destiny. His fate.

"More," Mikhail demanded into another kiss. Jin chuckled, and Mikhail whimpered at the movement of Jin lifting off him for a second. The action meant Mikhail lost his grip and instead grasped the wrought iron headboard with his hands. Something cold touched his stomach, and he opened his eyes. Jin was crouched between Mikhail's spread legs and concentrating on placing gems around him. The largest of deep red rubies, sapphires as big as a fist, diamonds in loose tumbling groups. Over him, around him. What was Jin doing? Why did the gems on his skin suddenly seem so hot to the touch. He gripped the headboard harder.

"So beautiful," Jin murmured. "And you are my greatest treasure," he added gently. Then he kissed Mikhail and left the siren-vampire in no doubt that Jin truly believed what he said.

Jin slicked his fingers, and bending over, he took the tip of Mikhail's cock into his mouth, before swallowing him almost to the root. The cavern of Jin's mouth was heat and texture, and Mikhail had to push his impending orgasm away ruthlessly. Cool lube touched his hole and Mikhail pressed against the fingers that Jin stretched him with. One, two, a third? Mikhail didn't know. The heat of the gems, Jin's tongue, and the heavy fullness of fingers preparing him were enough to have him demanding *now*.

"Please," he ordered. "Now."

Jin slid inside in a smooth move, bent over Mikhail with his eyes changing from white to the red of fire. The beast was there inside his locked gaze, but the man was Jin and he pushed deep and hard before retreating, then moving in again. Jin's control was evident in the expression of focus on his features.

"This will never end," Jin thought.

"Please," Mikhail begged in answer. *"More. Now."* Jin angled the push and Mikhail shut his eyes tight as his lover's cock pegged his gland. *"Once again, more."*

Jin leaned to rest his weight on one arm and closed the hand of the other around Mikhail's cock. Two twists of his fingers and Mikhail couldn't stop himself. He was going to come.

"Open your eyes," Jin demanded.

Mikhail opened them and stared up at the determination in Jin's face.

"My mate," Jin stated. "Do you want to be mine?"

Mikhail didn't stop to think. He had never in his long life experienced a connection like this, the white light cascading around them and glinting on the jewels.

"Yes… please… Yours… Mine." His words were incoherent, but when Jin pressed his lips to Mikhail's chest, fire seared into Mikhail. There was no pain, only the final step to completion.

Mikhail's orgasm ripped through him like wildfire, and Jin stiffened in his arms lifting his head to shout his pleasure at the exact same moment.

When Jin collapsed against him, Mikhail didn't even care that diamonds and rubies were caught between them. He welcomed the reminder of what had happened. The white strands around them coalesced into a ball of fizzing, popping heat. Then just as slowly as the light had formed, it thinned and vanished into Jin's skin.

"Mine," Jin said softly.

"Mine," Mikhail replied.

Everything was perfect. He was worthy of a mate. He was with Jin. Forever. Nothing could touch them.

Until…

Pain.

Intense, excruciating agony swelled in his chest and spread to every nerve in his body. He opened his mouth in a scream, and the last thing he focused on was Jin's fearful shout.

"No!"

. . .

JIN SCRAMBLED off of the bed and looked down in horror at his lover, who was thrashing on the bed. The dragon's design on his chest, left by the touch of Jin's breath and lips, was scarlet and tendrils of bright red grew and spread from the mark. This couldn't be happening. Where was the white? Mikhail was his fated mate. Jin's ancestors had blessed him and approved the union.

The door to the chamber flew open. A disheveled Bob leaped into the room, with Sam close behind.

"What happened?" Bob shouted. He was brandishing a dagger and his fangs had descended.

"We mated," Jin said, feeling powerless.

"Did it kill him?" Bob snapped. In seconds, he was at his friend's side and pushing aside the jewels that Jin had so lovingly used in the mating ceremony. Jin scooped the diamonds and held them tight. The only comfort was his hoard as his mate lay in front of him with the design spreading over the entire length of Mikhail from top to toe.

"The mark i-is nor-normal," Jin stammered. "White... No-not red. No pain..." He attempted to string together words, but nothing he was saying made sense. Mikhail shouldn't be feeling pain and the design should be white, a pale line in his smooth skin.

Bob shook Mikhail, then Sam joined him and pressed a hand to Mikhail's forehead.

"He's burning," Sam stated.

"Oh gods." Jin was helpless. "Save him."

"What do we do?" Bob demanded of Jin.

Jin thought quickly, then dropped his diamonds. Nothing was as important as Mikhail. He crawled to embrace his lover from behind and held tight. Mikhail immediately stopped moving.

"All of us," Jin said. "Touch him."

"What?" Sam looked confused and pulled his hand away. Immediately, Mikhail began to squirm in pain. Sam put his hand back and frowned when Mikhail once again lay still.

"What the hell?" Bob said. He crawled farther on the bed.

"His dragon soul needs to know where to come back to," Jin said gently. "I've never seen this, but centuries ago, when…" His voice trailed off. How did he make sense of the ancient stories and make them not sound like faery tales?

"Centuries what?" Sam prompted.

"I read that if the design burns, then there is the chance the mate will lose his way back to reality. I've never seen this."

"But it could happen? So why did you do it? Is it killing him?" Bob snapped angrily. Jin's heart broke. Mikhail was Bob's friend. Mikhail called Bob family.

"It shouldn't be this bad—uncomfortable, yes, but I can't sense his soul. My dragon must have been too powerful for him. I promise you I didn't know. How could I know? I never had any idea that I was…" Again Jin stopped. What was in his head made no sense. It couldn't be true. Eliza was the heir to the throne…

"You were what?" Bob asked with an edge to his voice.

"Heir to the throne of this kingdom."

The words hung there, and Bob opened his mouth to say something, then shut it just as quickly.

"Wha'appen?" Mikhail slurred. His waking stopped any more questions.

Jin's heart swelled with a curious mix of love, relief, and pride. His siren-vamp was a fighter. He said nothing to Mikhail—simply held tighter.

"You passed out," Bob said.

"Wow," Mikhail responded breathlessly. "That was some

orgasm." Then he blinked at Bob and Sam. "What are you doing in the room?"

Jin watched as both Bob and Sam moved away slowly as if they weren't sure they could stop touching Mikhail. When Mikhail just looked up at them sleepily then smiled, they made to leave. Bob stared directly at Jin and Jin nodded. The silent communication was evidently enough to have Bob satisfied he could go.

The door shut behind them, and Mikhail stretched luxuriously. The design had stopped spreading and was little more than a faint red line that curved and followed the muscled planes of his lover's chest. It would be there forever now. The gifts that came with it he would explain later. Right then, all Jin wanted was to hold Mikhail close and love him.

Certain that it was too soon to talk of love to his reluctant mate, he kept his silence. Mikhail snuggled closer and his breathing fell into a low, steady rhythm. He seemed unhurt by what had happened, and for that, Jin thanked the gods.

He tried to sleep, but he couldn't. There was so much spiraling in his thoughts. What had occurred couldn't be right. He wasn't a strong enough dragon to lead. He was a warrior, not a king.

What in hell was he going to do now?

MIKHAIL WOKE to an insistent banging in his head before realizing it was someone at the door. He stretched, then pushed against Jin, whose cock was hard and pressing into the small of Mikhail's back. With a sigh of contentment, he twisted in Jin's hold and came face to face with a sleepy smile from his new mate.

"So I lived, then," Mikhail joked. Jin frowned and kissed his forehead.

"You did," he said gently.

"Mikhail! Jin!" Bob's voice came through the wood. "We have a location. Leaving in ten."

In under five minutes, Mikhail had had the fastest shower on record. He noticed the pattern on his chest when he glanced in the mirror and admired it for a few seconds before pulling on yesterday's clothes. It was cool to be marked like this, and he was sure the symbols and lines meant something. After all this was over, he wanted to know what they meant. Jin waved a hand and he was clean and dressed. Mikhail envied him for a split second before focusing back on what they needed to do.

They joined Bob and Sam.

"The Osyth Pass," Sam said. "You know where that is?"

"I do," Jin replied quickly. Not only did he know the place, but strategically, it was as good a location as any for his lieutenant to kill Meel. Low in the southern caverns, it was what remained of an old diamond mine—huge networks of tunnels bored into the earth and one long bridge that joined it all. The disadvantage that Jin had was that Mikhail, Bob, and Sam had no idea what they faced. He stopped dead, and Mikhail walked into him.

Jin turned on his heel. "Will you stay here?" he asked Mikhail. "Where it is safe?"

Mikhail lifted an eyebrow with an expression that looked like he was not going to listen to reason.

Jin was one step away from taking his mate and locking him in a room. "Then, please, promise me that you'll stay to one side and let this be a dragon fight."

Mikhail looked mutinous for a moment, then relaxed. "We'll follow your lead," he finally said. Jin glanced at Bob and Sam, who eventually nodded in agreement, and he saw Bob link his hand with Sam's and squeeze it in reassurance.

Dragon against dragon in the huge caverns was Jin's job. There could only be one winner. This was a fight to the death.

Chapter Eight

SAM SHIVERED IN THE COLD STONE CHAMBER. WHY WERE HE and Bob even there anymore? They'd solved who had taken the girl. They knew Smoke had deceived the king and had handled kidnapping the princess. Sam's work was done. He wanted to go home and snuggle with Bob in his bed and plan his new bathroom.

He kicked a pebble in his path, watching as it spun away to collide with another.

"What's wrong, love?" Bob asked.

Sam sighed. "Can't we just go home?"

"Don't you want to save a kingdom?" Bob teased.

"Not particularly. Jin doesn't really need us for this and I wouldn't be much help against a dragon," Sam stated.

"We're here for moral support. Mikhail is a little freaked out over the dragon mate thing. You wouldn't abandon a friend in a time of need, would you?"

The 'yes' hovered on his tongue, but he couldn't say the word, not with Bob staring at him with such expectation.

"No." Sam dragged the word out from the bottom of his soul. Damn, when had he turned into such a softy?

Bob's hug pushed the air out of his lungs. "Bob, let go," Sam gasped. He received a smacking kiss on the top of his head before the vampire released him. Turning around, he found Jin and Mikhail staring at them.

"What?"

Jin shook his head. "Nothing. Are you coming? If you really don't want to come, I can fly you home."

Sam laughed. "There's no way I'm going anywhere on the back of a dragon."

They'd taken a car to the pass, and Sam planned to keep both feet entirely on the ground. Flying above the ground precariously perched on a dragon wasn't Sam's idea of a good time.

Jin snorted. "Then come along. I can smell them up ahead."

The group began moving forward again. Sam wondered how far these caves went. If diamonds were mined here, the tunnels could twist around forever. Luckily, they had a dragon guide. Sam didn't know if he could find his way out of there on his own.

Bob wrapped an arm around Sam's waist. "Stop worrying, love. I won't let anything happen to you."

Although he didn't know what Bob could do against dragons, Sam appreciated his lover's support.

Even with Jin declaring they were on the right path, it took a long time to trudge through what felt like miles of underground corridors. If Sam never entered another underground cavern in his life after this, he'd be extremely happy.

A loud scream sent a chill down Sam's spine. They started running. Sam had to catch himself from falling several times in the dark until he remembered he could summon a light. Still trying to catch up, Sam deliberately wished he could see. A glowing light appeared before him.

"How's it going, Sam?"

Sam screamed and clutched his chest.

Smudge, his familiar, wrapped his tail around his body. If a cat could look smug, Smudge pulled it off. "Don't do that. I've got to go, or I'll lose them."

He knew Bob wouldn't leave him, and Sam didn't want to be the one who slowed everyone down.

"You already did," Smudge declared, looking pointedly around the cavern. This part of the mine was a wider area that branched off into three other tunnels. Sam tried to listen and see if he could hear the others. *Where had Bob gone? He wouldn't leave Sam! Was their magic causing confusion?*

"How am I going to get out of this place?" Anxiety for his lover gripped him. What if the dragon killed Bob before Sam got there? For the first time since Bob had declared Sam his own, Sam wondered what life would be like without a pushy vampire trying to run his life. It only took a few seconds to realize that his life would be sad and lonely without his vampire. "Where did they go?"

"You can't hear them," Smudge said, flicking his tail.

"So I noticed. Wait, did you do something?" He didn't put anything past his pushy feline.

Smudge purred. *"I knew I did well when I chose you. I want you to be very careful, Sam. Smoke isn't anyone to trifle with. A dragon could easily kill even an enhanced human like you."*

"I'm not an enhanced anything," Sam snarled, "and I'm tired of everyone asking if I'm human. If paranormals have so many extra senses, how come they can never tell that I'm human?"

"I hate to break it to you, Sam, since you are so proud of

your humanity, but you aren't 100 percent human. Other creatures roam through your blood. In fact, so many different species are wrapped in your DNA, it has turned you to a human in appearance. You're probably the least human *human that I've ever encountered. I find you fascinating."* The cat's eyes glowed with interest, like he'd spotted a particularly juicy mouse.

Sam's stomach churned. "So that makes me what? The anti-human?"

"Don't be so dramatic," the cat scoffed. *"Most people would be pleased to learn they are more than they thought, not panicky."*

"Like you said, I'm not like most people. Am I even like any people?"

Smudge shook his head. *"You are unique, Sam Enderson. In my centuries on this Earth, I have never seen the likes of you. Come, we will join your comrades. They will be in trouble without us."*

A light flashed. When he had finished blinking, Sam saw that he now stood in the same chamber as the others.

"You okay?"

Bob's voice slid across Sam's mind like a welcome memory. He'd never been so happy for his boyfriend's intrusiveness before. *"Yeah, I'm fine now."*

"Hello, Smudge," Bob offered a tepid greeting. The familiar and the vampire didn't always see eye to eye on how they should deal with Sam.

"Smoke is on the other side," Jin said, pointing to the heavy wooden door blocking their path. "He's spelled the door somehow so we can't get through."

Before Sam could say anything else, Smudge sauntered forward. *"I'll take care of it."*

The familiar sat in front of the wooden barrier for a long

moment. Sam was about to ask Smudge if he needed anything when a pulse of power emitted from the creature. The door exploded off its hinges, narrowly missing Bob.

"Hey…" Bob growled.

"Sorry," Smudge replied in a tone Sam didn't think indicated any remorse at all.

With a glare at the feline, Bob stomped over to the entrance only to be stopped by Jin.

"Let me go in first," Jin said. "Dragons fighting dragons is much easier than scorched vampire."

Bob hesitated for a moment before nodding his agreement.

Sam let out a breath he hadn't known he'd been holding. What good were his supposed enhancements if he couldn't control his abilities?

"We'll talk later," Smudge said.

Sam wanted to yell at the cat, but that wouldn't change anything. He'd still be different.

Jin walked through the doorway, Mikhail following after. Sam paused a moment and exchanged worried glances with Bob when no sounds returned.

"We'd best follow," Bob said.

Sam nodded quickly.

Bob went before Sam as if he could protect Sam from any dangers. Since Sam often found himself in dangerous situations, Bob's sudden protectiveness made him smile.

He lost his happy expression when they entered the room. Sam covered his mouth to hold back a gasp.

They'd stepped into a large cavern. Sam didn't know how high the ceilings went since the darkness hid the top. An enormous altar covered one wall. It sparkled with an unnatural light. It took Sam a minute to realize that the altar was coated with thousands of diamonds. It would've been beautiful but for the body lying still on the top of it.

Meel lay spread out with a dagger through his heart. Blood poured off his body and dripped into the collection bowl beside him.

"I didn't want to do it," Smoke said. He raised his bloody hands as if to stave off their attack. The dragon appeared more upset than attacker. "He told me I could have the throne if I got rid of the princess. So I did that." He gestured at Meel's corpse. "Now he tells me I have to kill the king and the princess too. I'm not a murderer. I'm going to be a king!" Smoke shouted, waving his bloody hands.

If the dragon shifter was trying to persuade them to see his point of view, he was failing miserably. Even Sam, who didn't want to get involved in dragon politics, could tell the guy was unhinged.

"Who is he talking about?" Sam asked. He tried to keep his voice calm and low because they really were working with a crazy person. Best not to anger the guy who could plunge a knife into your heart. Feeling bad later didn't bring the dead guy back. Wait…

"Can you bring a guy back from the dead?" he asked his familiar.

"Not usually, no. Let me check on him."

Sam watched as Smudge kept to the shadows and trotted over to the body before sniffing it a few times.

"Get that thing away from us!" Smoke shouted. He leaned over the body of the king's brother. Sam swallowed at the sight of the blood all over the front of the dragon shifter's tunic.

"Why does it matter? You killed him," Sam muttered. The acoustics in this place were amazing and his voice echoed around the walls. He shrank back a little into the dark. Way to make himself obvious. Still, he didn't want to see his cat injured even if it was more a dangerous companion than a furry friend.

"I can kill you next," Smoke offered with a maniacal laugh. "You humans shouldn't be poking your nose where it doesn't belong."

"Finally, someone thinks I'm human!" Sam shouted his happiness, then quickly quieted as he realized it was completely inappropriate at that moment.

"Why the altar, Smoke? What are you into?" Jin asked. He was moving slowly toward the altar, and Sam had to admire the look of a predator cornering his prey.

"Talros said if I took over the dragon monarchy, he'd make sure I lived forever and had all the power I've craved. He would grant me the ability to lead my people. He lied, though. He keeps adding to the list of people who need to die. He lied!" Smoke screamed.

"Easy…" Jin soothed.

Sam saw Mikhail step forward while Jin tried to calm Smoke. Nothing like trying to distract a psychopath and check on the status of Meel at the same time.

Smoke huffed out a small flame to keep them at bay. "I don't trust you. I don't trust anyone. You are all liars." Smoke's voice took on the high-pitched edge of hysteria.

There would be no reasoning with the psychotic dragon, Sam could tell. Now they had to decide what to do about him.

Who's Talros?" Sam asked Bob through their link.

Bob shrugged.

"Who's Talros?" Sam asked out loud. If they were going to get to the root of this issue, they had to discover all the players.

Smoke made another hysterical giggle, an acrid stench puffing out of his nose like he'd turned rotten inside. He stepped away from Meel's body. "Talros is a necromancer. He's going to make me king, and I'll help him take over the world with his undead army."

Sam tilted his head as he studied the dragon. *Great.* He'd read about necromancers—wizards who concentrated on manipulating the dead. If Smoke was involved with one, there would be more trouble on the horizon. This could just be the beginning.

The unfocused gaze had him wondering if dragons could take drugs and what would be the right one to turn a dragon crazy?

Jin stepped closer and, in a swift move, took advantage of Smoke's hysteria and pinned him to the ground. Smoke struggled but stopped as soon as Jin extended wickedly curved talons and encircled Smoke's throat with them.

"And how the hell are *your* dragons going to live in a world populated by undead?" Jin shouted.

"He said I would have powers!" Smoke yelled back. "He wouldn't kill us."

"You want to make a deal with someone who wants to destroy everything? Didn't you consider why he was asking for your help?"

Sam exchanged a quick glance with Mikhail. Mikhail nodded then used the cover of great stone pillars to move closer to the altar while the dragons debated the merits of a partnership with a necromancer. Bob followed him, with Sam soon after. Sam didn't debate why they were moving closer. He just didn't want to let Bob out of his sight.

"What do you think?" Mikhail asked them.

"I think we're screwed if a necromancer is in on things now," Bob said. "He'll probably set all the paranormals against each other and bring them back to life after they kill each other." The entire idea sounded sick to Sam, but he had a good idea that that's what was happening.

Mikhail nodded. "Yeah, that's what I'm thinking too. We're going to have to capture Smoke and take him with us. The king will never believe this with his brother dead."

"Is he dead?" Sam asked.

With a careful eye on the arguing dragons, Sam sidled over to Meel's body. Blood dripped in a steady rate. He'd been filleted like a fish going to market. His guts splayed out as if Smoke had not only sliced him but had played with his intestines like a toy too. Sam quickly swallowed the bile rising in his throat.

"I can fix him," Smudge said.

"What?" Sam gratefully turned his attention to the cat.

"He's not completely gone yet. I can fix him, but there will be a price." Smudge narrowed his eyes at Sam. *"You might not like the cost."*

"What price?"

"I haven't decided yet."

Sam hesitated momentarily. Smudge was *his* familiar, and Sam should trust him. Right? He wouldn't do anything to put Sam in danger? Would he? Abruptly Sam decided he couldn't see someone die on his watch if he could stop it.

"*A* man's life is at stake. Save him!" Sam ordered. He'd worry about the consequences later. He couldn't waste time bartering with the familiar.

Smudge sighed, a strange sound from a feline. *"You will always follow your foolish heart no matter where it travels, won't you, Sam Enderson?"*

Sam blushed. "I don't think it's foolish to want to save someone."

"Not everyone deserves to be saved, Sam. Remember that." Smudge jumped up on the platform and hissed at the body lying there. A white whispery mist flowed out of his

mouth and drifted back to Meel. Sam stayed back a respectful distance, not wanting to distract the cat from whatever he was doing.

"What are you doing?" Smoke asked. He arched up under Jin's hold, but Jin wasn't letting go. "You can't do that. I have to take the body to the necromancer. He wanted a dragon, and I couldn't give him the princess." His gaze landed on Sam, his eyes red with fire and fury. "This is your fault, *human*. I'm going to make you pay for this."

Smudge's eyes glowed like twin suns. "If he needs a dragon so badly, he can have you!" The cat's voice echoed around the chamber as the familiar spoke out loud for the first time. In the middle of the chamber, a black hole opened. Sam watched in shock as an invisible force tore Jin away from Smoke and threw him against the nearest pillar. Then that same force sucked Smoke into the hole. A minute later nothing remained. No vortex. No dragon.

Sam cleared his throat. "Um, Smudge. If we don't know where the necromancer is, where did you send Smoke off to?"

The feline's smug expression worried Sam slightly. *"Where most necromancers hang out. The town cemetery. Now hush, I'm working."*

"Okay." Sam bit his thumbnail as he watched the cat.

He felt Bob, Mikhail, and Jin join him, but he didn't turn to look at them. He was too entranced with what the familiar was doing.

"What's he trying to attempt?" Jin asked.

"Cats are the keepers of the souls. He's giving Meel his soul back," Bob said. "Familiars are the only ones who can do that. Necromancers animate the body, but their corpses don't have souls. The cats charge a high price for returning a soul to someone."

Sam stiffened. A high price? What kind of a high price?

Oh crap.

"Sam. What did you promise that furry devil?" Bob asked.

"I don't know. He said there would be a price, but he didn't say what," Sam confessed.

Noises of disbelief came from the three men. "You don't make a deal with a familiar without set guidelines," Mikhail scolded. That sounded eerily familiar to Bob's last advice about not giving Sam's name to a witch, way back on day one as a detective. Why did advice always come so damn late?

"Yeah? Where were you five minutes ago?" *Now* they wanted to jump in to help. Sam ignored them as Smudge continued to work with Meel's soul.

"Sorry," Mikhail said.

"I never thought a soul had a form. It's interesting how you can see it," Sam commented, watching the silver wisps go from the cat to the dragon shifter.

"What do you mean??" Jin asked. He tilted his head to one side. "What can you see?"

Sam's heart sank. Not again. "The silver smoke going from Smudge to Meel. You can see it, right?"

Please let at least one of them agree. Three heads shook no.

Sam sighed. "Figures." He wasn't even going to discuss how Smudge thought he was all paranormals instead of no paranormals.

Bob squeezed Sam's shoulder. "We'll figure it out, love. Let's get Meel home, then we'll discuss what Smudge might have talked you into."

"Sure." Sam's heart sank. How did he always get himself into these situations?

A loud roar shook the cavern as Meel abruptly

transformed into his dragon form. A big red dragon stood before them for a minute before shifting back to human. Meel gave Sam a surprisingly graceful bow, considering the man didn't have a stitch of clothing on.

"I am in your debt, Sam Enderson," Meel said. "Your familiar has noted my debt to you and your future generations."

"Um, thanks," Sam said. He didn't know what future generations they thought he was going to produce, but the gesture was nice.

Smudge wrapped his tail around Sam's calves. *"We will speak of your debt to me later."*

"Great." Sam couldn't convey how excited he was at the prospect.

Chapter Nine

THE SMALL GROUP BEGAN TO MAKE THEIR WAY BACK through the caves in silence. Meel kept staring over at Jin, his gaze thoughtful. Mikhail didn't like the expression in Meel's eyes. When they entered the tunnels, Smudge disappeared with a twitch of his tail and a narrowing of his slanted green eyes. Bob and Sam had gone ahead, arguing in low voices about whatever deal Sam had entered into with Smudge. A promise to a familiar had you as good as tied up for eternity in one twist and turn after another. Mikhail wouldn't wish it on Sam. He only hoped that Smudge had different plans from the usual trickery that his kind played on those they chose to shadow.

"I want to thank you," Meel said softly. Mikhail looked over at him and saw he was addressing Jin.

"You have nothing to thank me for," Jin said quickly.

Jin sounded distracted and on edge and the heat from his body was palpable. He rolled his shoulders and glanced down at his hands, which still had the tips of his talons poking through the skin.

"What's wrong, Jin?" Mikhail asked.

"Everything feels wrong," Jin said sadly. "I thought I knew Smoke." He stopped in midstride and Mikhail stopped with him. Meel looked at the two of them but evidently considered it safer to walk with Bob and Sam. "He was a friend."

Mikhail reached out and placed a hand flat to Jin's chest. A faint white spark lit the small chamber briefly then died until they were just in the shadows cast by the torches on the wall again.

"I'm sorry," Mikhail said. "For what happened with Smoke, for the betrayal. It has to be hard." He only spoke the truth. Seemed to him dragons were big on family and the myriad links between generations. He slid his hand up and cupped Jin's face. Jin immediately rubbed his cheek against the touch. "What can I do to help?"

Jin pulled Mikhail close and linked his hands behind Mikhail's back to hold him tight. He buried his face into Mikhail's neck and the vampire shivered at the short blast of heat as Jin exhaled.

"Sorry," Jin muttered. "I don't know what is wrong with me. The fire inside me is pushing to get out."

"What causes that?"

"Puberty," Jin said on a laugh.

Mikhail chuckled alongside his lover. "I'm guessing puberty was a long time ago for you?"

"Just a bit. You wouldn't believe how destructive getting your fire can be. You should see how many fire dreams I had. I destroyed so many beds."

"So, we're ruling out the puberty-for-dragons stage. I think you're just confused and angry, and you feel betrayed." Mikhail nudged at Jin until *his* dragon lover lifted his head. "It's messing with you," Mikhail finished his assessment. "Some sleep, and an idea of what we're doing next about this whole necromancer thing and everything will be good."

"You think so?" Jin didn't sound convinced, but at least his voice held some hope that what Mikhail was saying was true.

"You should shift when we get topside and work off some of this heat," Mikhail teased. He pushed himself away and brushed at his shirt. "Because you are hot." He looked down to see two singe marks on the white material, and quickly looked up at Jin's horrified expression.

"What did I do?" Jin said fearfully. Mikhail could see Jin's clothes were intact—how was that possible? "Our clothes are spelled," Jin answered the unspoken question.

"So you're burning up. A lot."

"Let's keep walking. I think what you said about shifting is good," Jin forced out between gritted teeth. He didn't look well, his eyes half closed and a sheen of sweat coated every available part of his skin. They restarted the journey back, and Mikhail hurried them as much as he could. His chest was tight and his breathing labored. Damn tunnels ran sometimes at forty-five-degree angles, and he was clearly not as fit as he'd thought. He sighed in relief when the last tunnel flattened and they were almost out. A sharp pain knifed through Mikhail, and he doubled over with his hands on his thighs.

"Mikhail?" Sam and Bob hovered. Sam touched a hand to his back. "Talk to me. Are you okay?"

Jin growled low in his throat and the sound echoed in the tunnel. "I have to… I… have to… go…" he forced out. "Wa-watch him…" He stumbled out toward the light at the end of the tunnel and vanished around the corner. Mikhail straightened and placed a hand on the wall to steady himself. "Let me get my breath back," Mikhail said.

"You look like hell," Bob commented.

"Thanks for that, Bob," Mikhail deadpanned. The pain had eased. No doubt it was part of some new crazy link he had to his lover.

Meel joined them and hovered uncertainly. His portly face was red with exertion, but he wasn't throwing off heat like Jin. Evidently he wasn't affected by whatever had Jin burning.

"There have been other murders, you know," he said. Mikhail wondered if the older dragon had a point to what he was saying and focused in on the words. "Ten years ago, my older brother Cedric was murdered. He was second in line for the throne."

"So you were third? I'm guessing you were the first suspect in your brother's murder," Sam suggested. "What was it? Did you want the throne and thought removing brother two moved you up in the pecking order?"

Meel shook his head. "You don't understand. The throne isn't a birthright. The ancients choose a new ruler based on brave acts and selflessness and generosity, and for having the heart of a king. Over time, it has tended to go from one royal to the next, but it isn't preordained. I am the history keeper. I record the bloodlines. I'm not a king in waiting. The king has been on the throne so long many of our people have forgotten how the throne is passed down. Fate chooses who next takes the seat of power."

"So could Jin be right when he says he may possibly be an heir?"

"I know what we will find when we are home," Meel said randomly. His words rambled, and he had a glazed expression that disintegrated in grief.

"You're not making any sense," Bob said.

"When the king was younger, many centuries ago, he

nearly died in battle... He was close to death, and his heir was marked with the design of the dragon king, ready to take his place." Meel touched his throat and ran a finger from there to his chest right over his heart. "Cedric was chosen as the heir, and he was ready to take the king's place if he had to."

"Your brother, the middle one," Mikhail summarized.

"When he got the mark, he..." Meel stopped and looked suddenly scared.

"What?" Mikhail snapped. "Tell us what happened?"

"He burned hot, but he wasn't needed—the king survived. The mark never left, though. Once the ancients choose you, that is your fate, your destiny. Cedric had that mark until the day he was murdered. They never found his killer."

"You think it was Smoke?" Sam asked curiously. "That he has been slowly removing heirs in his way to the throne?"

Mikhail wanted to talk about the issue of Jin burning hot, but he patiently waited until Meel formed an answer to Sam's question.

"Smoke is... was... a brave and strong dragon. His bloodline is pure and respected in the clutch. He could assume that if he cleared the path of enough dragons he could be king. So maybe he did kill Cedric."

"Smoke wanted to kill Eliza," Mikhail pointed out in support. "He thought she could be an heir."

"She's a child, hardly brave and strong yet," Bob said.

"You didn't see her face down the sirens," Mikhail interrupted. "Can you tell me what happened when Cedric received the mark as heir?"

"He burned hot..." Meel repeated. Then he appeared to be lost in thought. Mikhail opened his mouth, ready to ask the dragon to get to the point, but shut it again at a frown from Bob. Finally, Meel continued, "When he shifted from dragon to man, his chest had a design that matched that of his fated mate, a beautiful violet dragon from another clutch."

Mikhail pulled aside his singed shirt. "You mean like this kind of mark?"

Meel looked, then closed his eyes tight.

"Meel?" Sam prodded the prince's arm.

"Yes. Like that. If Jin is burning and the design appears, it can only mean one thing. The king is near death, or is dead."

Mikhail shook off the pain and the feeling of breathlessness. "We need to get to the king." No one argued, and they hurried to get out into the fresh air, to the car, then on toward the throne room.

JIN LANDED CLUMSILY and curled his wings around himself. Somehow he had lost any grace he'd had and couldn't sustain flight for long with pain coursing through him. What was wrong? He shifted to man and slumped to the grass but didn't bother dressing. He was so damn hot and the fire itched under his skin.

"Are you okay?" Nillon's voice came from his left. His brother sat down next to him with his back to a large rock. "What happened?"

"Nothing," Jin said tiredly.

"The last time I saw a crash landing like that, the dragon was dragging a top-heavy bag of rubies." He peered at Jin. "I don't see any rubies."

"I just feel..." Jin stopped. Nillon was his brother, and misguided as he had been in believing Jin was the bad guy, he was, at the core, a gentle soul. "Tired," he finished.

"You look tired," Nillon agreed.

"Thanks, brother," Jin deadpanned. Nillon huffed a laugh,

then leaned back and began blowing lazy smoke rings into the air.

"So, he is your mate then," Nillon said finally. "That vampire-siren hybrid of yours."

"Mikhail," Jin offered. He waited for more.

"So what is that thing there, then?"

"What?" Jin asked. He didn't know what Nillon was talking about.

Nillon gestured at him. "That."

Jin followed the direction that Nillon was pointing in and blinked as he took in the intricate design that had appeared on his chest, and down one arm. Black and gold, it curled and looped in the shape of a dragon with wings spread and was similar in design to Mikhail's. All except that his had extra lettering that spread down to his wrist in a complicated pattern. The dragon's mate, in his case Mikhail, had a mark to show that fate had placed them together. A dragon was only marked when...

Sudden horror washed over Jin.

"What?" Nillon said urgently as Jin scrambled to stand and magicked clothes onto his body.

"The king's mark," Jin said. "That is the only reason we have these..."

In tandem, the two shifters sprinted to the gate and into the palace. In minutes, they were inside and faced with the two dragons responsible for controlling entrance to the throne room and the king's private chambers.

"Let us in," Jin ordered.

They didn't even argue—evidently a burning Jin was a forceful Jin. They pushed inside, and the horror of what met them had Jin sliding to a halt. The king was dead, his throat cut and his form half shifted to dragon in a grotesque twisted shape. Next to him, unconscious and lying in some of her father's blood, was Eliza. Nillon immediately scooped Eliza up and held her close. She was injured. Whoever had killed the king had felt it important to remove Eliza as well.

"She's breathing," he said. "And healing."

Jin fell to his knees next to the king. Instinct had him checking for a pulse, but there was no sign of life, and the king was ice cold. Jin reached inside, but the emptiness inside the shell of the body was absolute—there was no spark of life.

"He's gone," Jin said in anguish. He sat back on his heels and let up a mighty roar that shook the room, half shifting to dragon and allowing the grief of the entire clutch to have a focus.

"Do you think she saw?" Nillon asked brokenly. Jin looked up at his brother. "Gods, I hope not." He pulled at the drapes and tore one down—it would have to do as a temporary shroud. Gently he placed it over the king's form, attempting to give the dragon some semblance of dignity in death.

"Jin!" Mikhail's voice came from behind him, and Jin had never been happier to hear his mate. He retracted his wings and forced his fangs and claws to retreat before he turned to face his lover. He stood in a smooth movement and held out a hand. Mikhail didn't argue—he crossed to hold Jin's hand tightly. Intense white light engulfed them momentarily, then dissipated. Abruptly Jin had the weight of his destiny thrust upon him.

He was king.

Chapter Ten

"ELIZA'S RESTING," SAM ANNOUNCED. SAM HAD SETTLED THE princess in her bed while Mikhail, Bob, and Jin had spread the news about the king's death. They had yet to announce Jin as the new king. Hopefully, they could keep it quiet for a while longer. The dragons would start circling soon to make sure Jin would make a good ruler, and Jin wasn't quite ready to grab the reins of leadership.

"Good. She needs her sleep," Jin said. "She's healing and she's had a shock over her father."

Jin would make sure the princess got everything she needed. Instead of being isolated in a group of grown dragons, he would find her some friends.

"Do you think she'd like that school you sent your girl to?" Jin asked. From Bob's description, it sounded like a nice place.

Sam scowled. "She just lost her father and you're sending her away."

Jin shook his head. "You don't understand. Dragon children are rarer than purple rubies. The clutch could judge her for not being the next in line for the throne. They'll look for flaws because the gods didn't choose her. Someone has already hurt her. I want her safe. There will be less pressure if she's someplace away from the mountain where she can make some non-dragon friends. The more connections she can make inside and outside the mountain, the better she'll adjust as an adult. We isolate ourselves and I don't want that for Eliza."

"That's a good idea," Bob said, ignoring the glare from his mate. "I'd be happy to put in a word with the schoolmaster. I don't think they'd have a problem with a dragon shifter as long as Eliza signed their code of conduct that states you can't use your powers against other students. It's grounds for immediate expulsion."

"Fair enough." Jin could see how a school full of mixed paranormals could be a problem if they were all using their powers against each other. He had no doubt some probably did so on the sly, but Eliza could hold her own.

"Could you guys give us a few minutes?" Mikhail asked.

"Sure," Sam grabbed his vampire's arm and dragged him down the hall. "Come find us when you're ready to go hunt down Smoke."

Jin shifted from foot to foot. He knew Mikhail would be angry with him. Putting off this confrontation wouldn't be in his best interest. The anxiety pouring off of Mikhail itched at him like a bad rash.

"Don't think you can escape this conversation," Mikhail said. "You can't be king. I can't be mated to a king."

An edge of hysteria filled Mikhail's voice.

"Easy, love." Jin took Mikhail's hands in his own. "It'll be all right."

"No, it won't." Mikhail shook his head frantically. "I've been royalty before. It hasn't worked out."

Jin cupped Mikhail's face. "I'm not like your father, and

I'm not a siren. I love you, Mikhail. If I could give up the crown, I would. The only way to give it up now is through death."

The panic in Mikhail's eyes tore at Jin's heart.

"I don't know if I can go through that again," Mikhail said. "I mean, I know you can't give up being king, but I don't know if I can be your partner."

Jin wrapped Mikhail in his arms and held him close. "I can't live without you. We are bound."

Mikhail snuggled into Jin's embrace. Despite his reservations, he obviously still wanted Jin.

"I don't know what to do," Mikhail confessed.

"Stay with me. I need you." Jin didn't have words to convey how much he had to have Mikhail in his life. Mikhail and air were the two necessities he couldn't live without.

Mikhail gripped Jin's shirt. "I'm afraid."

"Take a chance on us. I can't promise to be a perfect mate, but no one will ever work harder to make you happy."

After a long moment, Mikhail nodded. "I'll give us a try."

Jin smiled. "Good."

Sam rushed back toward them with Bob at his heels. "Sorry to interrupt. We need to go. Smudge just told me the necromancer is at the cemetery. This might be our only chance to catch him."

Jin glanced around but didn't see the familiar. "Where is Smudge?"

"He went back home. He said he can't do anything to help against a necromancer," Sam said. "Something about incompatible magic."

Jin wished he could just go back home when things became too difficult. Grabbing Mikhail and holding him tight sounded a lot better than dealing with a psychotic necromancer trying to destroy dragonkin.

"What can we do?" Mikhail asked the question Jin had wondered about. If a powerful familiar couldn't or wouldn't fight, how could they defeat one?

Bob stepped forward. "Let's go see. We have to stop him, no matter what. We won't know what's possible until we check out this guy ourselves. He seems to work behind the scenes so far, and has his minions do all the work."

Jin couldn't argue with that logic. The necromancer had used Smoke as his way into the dragon mountain. Jin wondered who else might be under the necromancer's control. He might not have always got along with Smoke, but he'd never have suspected him to be a traitor.

"I'll leave Nillon and Meel in charge. Even if he isn't the next king, Meel is a powerful influence in the dragon kingdom and the others will listen to him. As far as everyone knows, he's the new king. Let's not disillusion them until we get back."

Jin didn't mention that Meel could still be the new king if their battle didn't work out.

Mikhail smacked his arm. "I heard that," he snarled.

"Not saying it out loud doesn't make it less true," Jin said.

"Doesn't make what true?" Sam asked.

"Nothing," Mikhail said. "Let's go. We can worry about dragon kingdoms after we take care of Smoke and his psychotic master."

Jin agreed. First, deal with the necromancer, then work on their relationship. He didn't know which one was scarier.

SAM CAST a nervous glance around the cemetery. Why didn't they just cue the creepy music and be done with it? The dark sky, the light mist swirling around their feet, and the tombstones decorating the ground could've come straight from a horror movie.

"Are you looking for your friend?" a dry, raspy voice asked as the stench of rotting eggs and turned earth wafted to them.

Fear trickled up and down Sam's spine. He hadn't been this frightened during the siren attack or when he'd faced down an evil dragon or even when he'd walked into a werewolf bar and demanded answers.

None of those creatures had exuded evil like the owner of the raspy voice slithering across his eardrums. Only Bob's reassuring presence beside him stopped Sam from bolting. He wouldn't abandon his lover no matter how infuriating he usually found him.

Slowly, along with his friends, Sam turned around and discovered he hadn't really known true fear until that moment.

Seven feet tall, the necromancer towered over the four of them. Papery-looking blue-tinged skin stretched across a skeletal face as if the being had already died once and hadn't completely returned to its previous humanity.

"Necro-puppet," Bob whispered into Sam's brain. *"Not the necromancer himself—a minion."*

"Oh."

That made more sense. The necromancer wouldn't put himself out there for attack. He'd simply send another to do his bidding. Sam searched the area but saw no sign of Smoke.

"Are you looking for someone?"

A sinking feeling plunged into Sam's chest. He knew he wouldn't like the answer he was about to receive.

"What did you do with Smoke?" Jin asked before Sam could get the words out. A spurt of relief wiped out a bit of Sam's anxiety. He wasn't in a hurry to look into the creature's soulless eyes. Did it make him a coward to not want to be noticed by whatever this blue thing was?

Bob wrapped an arm around Sam's waist. "It'll be all right, love. We'll do what we usually do." Bob whispered.

"Hope a demon will come by and burn everyone down?" Sam replied in an equally quiet voice.

Bob's laughter beside him melted the ice encasing Sam's body. With his lover at his side, they had to win. He wouldn't accept any other possibility.

"I have what is left of your buddy Smoke," the creature said. He threw something at them. It bounced off a headstone before skidding to a halt in the middle of their group.

At first, Sam didn't understand what he was seeing. Then he almost hurled.

Smoke's claw lay on the bed of dead leaves. Someone had chopped Smoke's hand off while he was in dragon form.

"What happened to the rest of him?" Jin asked.

"Do you really want to know?" The creature smiled, revealing bloody, sharp teeth.

Sam pressed a hand to his stomach, willing it not to heave and disgrace him.

"Easy, babe." Bob sent Sam reassuring thoughts, keeping the nausea at bay.

"You are an abomination who should be sent back to hell!" Jin shouted.

Sam could feel Jin's pain slamming into him in big waves. Smoke might have betrayed the dragon king, but they'd had a long history of friendship before that.

"You think you can send me there, little dragon? You and your vampire friends?" The creature laughed. His dead eyes swept over to Sam. "And what are you?"

Sam sighed. Even the creepy undead dude didn't buy his human statement. He wondered if Smudge would miss him once he was eaten. Hopefully, the familiar would at least feel a twinge of remorse over abandoning Sam to his fate.

"I'm human," Sam said. Maybe if he said it enough times, it would turn back to being true.

The creature tossed back his head and laughed, a loud, booming sound surprisingly robust compared to his almost whispery voice. "You fool no one with that story, supposed-human." It shrugged. "Never mind. You will die in the end."

Jin's flame stopped that line of reasoning. The creature screamed, batting at his clothing. "You will pay!" it screeched.

Without warning, the creature jumped at Jin and slashed at him with claws that slid out of the tops of his fingers.

Jin's scream echoed in the night. He spat more fire at the beast as he tumbled back to the ground. Mikhail sang a piercing siren song that had Bob hitting the ground. Even Jin looked unsteady, and Sam thought dragons could defeat anyone. Sam stood there, unsure of what to do. He foolishly didn't have a weapon. The beast knocked Mikhail over, and the siren-vampire hit a tombstone before falling still. Sam froze as the beast turned to him.

Sam's mind raced over different possibilities. What could he do? "I wish I had a light," he whispered.

A glowing ball appeared between Sam and the beast.

"No." The beast swiped at the ball, screaming when his hand flowed through it. "I'll kill you, fake-human."

Sam took a careful step back, searching for anything to help. The beast appeared blinded by the light, unable to see Sam through the brilliance.

Still, it wasn't enough to save him. Sam didn't know how much longer the light would hold. Sam's eyes fell on his bracelet. Without further thought, he wrapped his hand around the band and closed his eyes.

"Help me," he whispered. He didn't know how the band worked, but he hoped one of the entities who had promised to come to his aid was paying attention.

A loud boom rocked the cemetery. Sam's feet were knocked out from under him as the trio of fae came out of nowhere and placed themselves between the creature and Sam. With their tattooed faces and silver eyes flashing with light, they formed an impressive barrier.

"We are displeased you have tried to harm our Sam," the fae said in one voice.

The creature growled. Sam climbed to his feet but stayed where he was, not too proud to let the fae handle this fight. He couldn't stand up against this spawn of the necromancer, not when it could down a dragon.

Sam knew the limit of his abilities, and he'd be dead before he destroyed this creature.

"You think you can defeat me?" the necro-puppet sneered.

The middle fae lifted his hand and the creature disintegrated. One moment he was a hissing, spitting, snarling threat, the next a pile of ashes on the floor. As one, the trio turned back to Sam. Their eyes glowed as they examined him.

"Are you all right, Samuel Enderson?" the fae on the left said.

"Yes, thank you," Sam replied.

"You are welcome. Let us know if there is anything else you need," the fae on the right said. Before he could say anything else, the trio vanished.

He didn't think he'd ever get used to their strangeness.

A low groan had Sam rushing to Bob's side. "Are you okay, love?"

Bob blinked up at Sam as if trying to get him into focus. "Those fae came again?"

"Stop reading my mind. How many times do I have to tell you, it's rude?" Sam scolded.

"It's Mikhail's fault. He scrambled my brain with his siren song," Bob grumbled.

Sam decided to let this one slide.

Matching moans from behind him alerted Sam to Mikhail and Jin coming back around. Sam helped Bob to his feet. "So the fae took care of the necromancer's creature?"

Sam nodded. "Yeah, but we still don't know where the necromancer came from or where he lives. He'll still be able to terrorize the dragons."

"Or you. If he knows you're the reason the fae destroyed his minion, then he might come after you next," Bob reasoned.

"Perhaps," Sam agreed. "But I doubt I'm interesting enough to be a target."

Jin helped Mikhail to his feet and approached the pair, patting Sam on the back.

"Don't underestimate yourself, Sam. You are plenty interesting," Jin argued. "The dragonkin are forever in your debt for not only rescuing our princess but for stopping their king from being necromancer fodder."

Sam laughed. "You're welcome."

Jin pulled a silver wisp of magic out of the air and touched Sam's bracelet. The tiny amount of smoke cleared and left behind the small design of a little dragon breathing fire.

"Okay," Sam said. He couldn't help sounding cautious but he tried hard to hide the disquiet swishing through his body. He had to get a grip on his relationship with other paranormals. Either they were friends or they were foe, and he had enough enemies at this time.

"Mikhail and I are going back to the mountain. I'm going to ask around and find out if anyone knew who Smoke hung out with. Surely someone saw him with this necromancer," Jin said.

"Sam and I will search the area for clues," Bob said before Sam could reply.

"Good. If you find anything, let us know." Jin wrapped an arm around Mikhail. "I will fly Mikhail home."

Mikhail's mouth dropping open didn't make Sam believe the vampire-siren liked that plan, but it wasn't for him to intercede. If Mikhail didn't say anything, Sam wouldn't. Bob stifled a laugh beside him.

"We'll contact you," Bob offered.

"Could you also let me know how things go with Mal's school?"

"Sure," Sam spoke up. Why did he feel like he should join the PTA and carpool?

Jin transformed before their eyes. Mikhail climbed onto his back, his slow motions revealing his nerves.

"He'll be fine," Bob reassured Sam.

"Are you sure Jin won't drop him?" Sam asked.

"I'm sure. Jin would never let his mate fall." Bob sounded confident in his assessment. Sam relaxed.

After the pair took off, Sam and Bob spent the next hour scouring the cemetery. They came across nothing unusual past the pile of ashes.

"That was a waste," Sam grumbled. So far this had been the worst case ever. Although they'd rescued the girl and the prince, in the end the king had died. And now it looked as if Mikhail was staying to be the king's consort, or whatever his title would be. Sam would miss Mikhail. The beautiful vampire had proved to be a good friend more than once. What would Bob do without his best friend?

"Hey, he'll be fine, and I'll be fine too," Bob assured him. He squeezed Sam's arm in a show of comfort.

"I know. Jin really likes him," Sam said. He knew the dragon would take good care of Mikhail. It didn't make it any easier, though.

They took one last look around before heading back to the castle.

Epilogue

THE JOURNEY AWAY FROM THE CASTLE WAS SLOW AND BORING without the urgency they had felt in getting to the dragonkin home. They stopped after a couple of hours at a diner and filled up on non-dragonkin food. Eating normal junk food was a relief after eating food that had been charred to hell and back.

Bob wandered off to check perimeters and Sam walked outside to the picnic area. He sat at the first table he came to and lifted his face to the sky, the late afternoon sun warming his skin.

"I thought it best to discuss this here before you get home." The voice was low and firm. "I'd rather we didn't include your menagerie in our discussions."

Sam sighed. He'd known Smudge would find him sooner or later. He just hoped it would be when they were at home, and when Bob was next to him.

"Hello," he said carefully. He straightened in his seat and located Smudge sitting in the shade of the picnic table. "What menagerie?" he asked, then wished he hadn't.

Smudge sniffed. "The see–through, whiny ghost, the

concrete thing on your desk, not to mention the killer spiders in your attic."

"Spiders. Killer." Sam blinked at the sudden loathing and fear curling inside him. "I have killer spiders in my attic?"

Smudge yawned widely, showing her tiny pointed teeth. "They're only babies, no bigger than a dinner plate."

"I don't like spiders," Sam said desperately.

"And I don't like ghosts, or gargoyles, but I have to live with them," Smudge said, sounding bored.

"How many spiders?" Sam asked.

"I lost count," Smudge said with what looked like a definite smirk. "Anyway, the birds will kill them for you."

"What birds?"

"The ones coming to stay," Smudge said. He sounded like he thought Sam was stupid or something. Sam wasn't stupid. He was confused. Maybe he had sunstroke.

"I have birds coming to stay?"

"And cats, and some dogs maybe, although we'll need to keep them separate."

"I'm not following."

"There may be a couple of frogs," Smudge added thoughtfully.

"What would you say to starting from the beginning?"

"I am here to explain how you will fulfill your promise to me. You're to provide a place to stay for unmatched familiars in need of a paranormal until you find a match for them," Smudge said, flicking his tail.

"A place. Match..." Sam wasn't able to string together a coherent sentence. He already had a ghost, a gargoyle, and apparently killer spiders. He was not adding dogs, cats, and—wait... birds?—to his household. He imagined dogs chasing cats chasing pigeons chasing spiders, and he buried his face in his hands and groaned.

"So it's agreed then." The crack in the air accompanied the words, and Sam didn't even look to know that Smudge had gone. By the time Bob sauntered around the corner whistling like he didn't have a care in the world, Sam had managed to calm himself down a little.

"Do you like pets?" Sam asked.

Bob looked curious at the question "Pets? I had a hamster once."

Sam snorted a laugh. He couldn't imagine big, bad vampire Bob owning a hamster. "Smudge was here."

Bob scented the air, and he wrinkled his nose. "Oh," he said helpfully. "What was he asking for?"

"He's going to be using my place as some kind of halfway house for unmatched familiars." He shook his head and allowed Bob to help him to his feet.

"That's not so bad," Bob said gently. "Together, we can handle anything."

Together sounded really good.

AFTER THE REST STOP, Sam felt fidgety and one thought kept pushing at the base of his neck. He felt like his skin was too tight and his chest hurt. The band of tension around his head had a bad headache threatening. Every time he closed his eyes, he saw horrible images of gravestones and zombie-like creatures rearing up from the mud with gaping mouths and claw-like hands. It was awful, and with an insistent prickle, fear twisted with anxiety curled inside him, making him uneasy. Bob picked up on the tension immediately.

"Sam? What's wrong?" he asked.

"I'm surprised you can't read my mind and see for yourself," Sam snapped irritably, then immediately felt bad.

Bob casting a quick glance at him in surprise didn't help. "Sorry," Sam said quietly. He didn't want Bob seeing the horror that was in his thought. "My head hurts. I feel muddled. I don't know what's wrong with me, I just feel..." He shrugged.

"What we've just been through, add in Smudge and the promise, and I'm not surprised you're shaken."

"It isn't that," Sam said instantly. "We can't waste time worrying about what happened before, and, like you said, we'll deal with Smudge together. It's Mal. I can't help feeling something is wrong. I know I'm just being stupid. She's at school and she's fine."

They drove a few miles more before the silence in the car became too much. Sam's head was a mass of worst case scenarios, all of which centered on Mal or Bob.

"Let's go visit the school," Bob finally said.

Sam couldn't believe the relief he felt. "Thank you," he said simply.

Bob patted his knee. "You should always listen to your fears and go with your instincts," he said.

Sam waved his hands in front of him and put on a deep voice. "For that is the vampire way..." he said.

Bob smiled at him. "*I love you, Sam.*"

Sam smiled in return. He would never get tired of hearing that from his sexy, infuriating, bossy vampire lover. "*I love you, too.*"

They reached the beginning of the long road to the school as dusk darkened the sky with smudges of purple and navy. The nearer they got, the edgier Sam got. What if the necromancer was at the school? What if they should have brought a dragon with them? Or a fae? Or an army of anyone they could find. If the necromancer was controlling that necro-puppet, then he would have seen Sam, seen what Sam could conjure in the way of help. Had he put his family in danger? Where was Smudge?

"Smudge? Can I get some help?" Nothing. He fingered the bracelet. A part of him wanted to demand help from someone, anyone, but he didn't know why.

When they finally reached the gates, nothing seemed out of the ordinary. There were no bodies on the floor, or piles of ash or fire, and he couldn't sense peril. Of course, as a normal human, he wouldn't *see* peril even if it stood up and poked him between the eyes. They parked the car, and Bob was up and out in seconds. He waited for Sam, who left the car a lot slower. The weight of dread that lay on Sam like a cloak was impossible to push away.

"I can't go in," he said frantically as breathing became difficult. He leaned on the car and bowed his head. Sickness rolled inside him.

"Talk to me, Sam." Bob placed a hand on his arm, and the reassurance of it had Sam able to get his breathing back to an approximation of normal.

"Sam! Bob!" Mal's voice echoed in the courtyard inside the gate, and she threw herself bodily at Bob. Then reached out to pull Sam in for the hug. "You came!"

"Sam heard you, so of course we came," Bob said firmly.

Sam was confused. What did Bob mean?

"I tried to talk to you as well, but it didn't work, so I sent messages out to Sam." She beamed proudly.

"Sam said he had to come visit," Bob agreed. He sounded just as proud.

"Wait. You were sending me images of reanimated people with rotting faces?" Sam said incredulously.

Bob raised an eyebrow, and Mal punched Sam in the arm. "No, silly," she said with a laugh, "I just sent you a message about coming to visit."

Then why did I see rotting bodies when I closed my eyes?

"Mr. Enderson! Mr. Vampire!" Sam turned to face the owner of the new voice. The principal was scurrying across the courtyard as fast as her heels would allow her—her pearls swinging dangerously from side to side.

"Ms. Triplewine," Bob said cordially. Sam nodded his hello because his head was going to burst if he spoke.

"We have a problem with the boiler," she said quickly.

"We're not plumbers," Bob explained carefully. Sam leaned against Bob and closed his eyes. He could listen—he just wasn't able to talk. "We're detectives."

"Oh my goodness," Ms Triplewine twittered. She fluttered her hands in front of her and giggled nervously. "I don't need a plumber, I have one of those. No, I need…" She lowered her voice. Sam half opened his eyes, and the principal leaned in closer. Sam could smell peppermint and sage and something else that was cloying and thick. He gagged but managed to hold the action in. "Big strong detectives like you and Mr. Enderson." She pressed her hand on Bob's arm.

"Why do you need a detective?" Sam managed to force out. He coughed at the effort, and Mal clambered from Bob's arms to his. Just the clean scent of her and the happiness she exuded was enough to calm him a little.

"There have been noises," she said conspiratorially. "Banging. Moaning. It started a few days ago. I must admit, it's somewhat unsettling for the students and staff."

"We don't deal with banging and moaning," Bob said. Sam wondered how his lover could keep a straight face.

"This is why I called you both," Mal said. "I heard the noises and I went to look—"

"I told her not to," Ms. Triplewine interrupted.

"I saw things," Mal said.

"What kind of things?"

"Like…" She stopped and wriggled until she stood on the ground. She held her hands out in front of her and walked stiff-legged, letting out the odd moan. "Like that," she said as she came to a stop.

"I'm sorry to say, and this has never happened in the seventy years I have been principal, that we appear to have a zombie infestation."

Sam blinked. Bob stood with his mouth open. Mal grinned in delight. Ms. Triplewine just looked horrified at what she had just said.

"Okay," Bob said finally. "So you need to know why, who, what, and how to deal with the infestation."

"Exactly," she said. She sounded encouraged by what Bob was saying with such confidence. Sam wished he felt as happy. The images he was being shown were not cute vampire kids playing zombie. These were rotting flesh, and wild eyes, and teeth ripping and… God. They had to turn this case down. But Mal was at the school. So did they take her out of her classes?

Evidently, Bob had the same thoughts. He sighed heavily, then pulled Sam close in a hug.

"Looks like we have our next case."

THE END

THE CASE OF THE

Sinful Santa

Chapter One

"WHAT DO YOU KNOW ABOUT ZOMBIES?" SAM STARED straight at Bob as he asked the question, hoping his mate would have some insight.

Bob frowned. "I know as much as you do."

"I looked it up," Ms. Triplewine, the school's principal, said excitedly. She handed Bob a book that was little more than two inches by two inches. Sam didn't like to point out that he doubted there could be much in the tiny book that could help them.

Bob accepted the book carefully, ignoring her shy smile. Sam groaned inwardly. Mal's head teacher was so far gone on Bob she didn't even try to hide it. Sam sat on the ground, trying to pull oxygen into his lungs. An invisible weight or something was pushing on his chest. He tried to take long slow breaths to gather more air into his lungs, but his vision sparkled a bit around the edges.

Bob crouched in front of him, "I'm not sure you should be here." He placed a hand flat on Sam's forehead. Sam tilted his head into the touch, encouraging more contact.

"Maybe it's the zombies," Mal said helpfully. "Affecting Sam," she added.

Sam wasn't sure what was causing this. The net of despair that settled over him was stifling and he felt nauseous. If it was the zombies then they needed to deal with them. He reached for the book, but Ms. Triplewine grabbed his hand.

"Humans can't touch the book," she said shrilly. "It's spelled and for you to touch it would mean an immediate and bloody death."

Sam snatched his hand back, then rested his face in his palms. Exhaustion beat at him. He hadn't been sleeping the last few nights with visions of zombies stalking through his dreams. "Open the book, Bob, find out what we need to do so the three of us can all go home."

"I'm not going home," Mal announced. "I love it here."

Sam raised his head. He wasn't going to argue with Mal —he'd let Bob talk to her about this one. Sam knew he and Bob would be on the same page.

"It's okay, sweetie," Bob said as he hugged her. "You don't have to leave. When we clear out the zombies, 'everything will be back to normal."

"Thanks, Dad," Mal said.

So much for solidarity.

Sam couldn't even find it in himself to argue. He'd just grab Mal and they'd all leave. Find a school that didn't have the walking dead in their basement. That didn't stop him from sending his lover a dirty look.

Bob opened the tiny book, which looked like something made for a doll when he held it in his big, capable hands. He thumbed through it and peered at the writing.

"It's miniature," he said with a frown. "Something in the writing about angels and demons. I can't make it out."

"Demons?" Sam latched onto the single word. They knew a demon. "We should call Danjal."

"We can't," Bob said. "Remember, he and Hartman are on holiday in the mountains."

"Then who do we call?" Sam snapped. He immediately apologized, "Sorry, I feel like death."

He fingered the patterns on his bracelet. Was there a charm here that could help? Maybe one from the fae or vampires. Inspiration hit him. "Maybe we should get Smudge here. He'd know…"

A snap in the air accompanied by the smell of ozone heralded Smudge's arrival. He appeared right beside Sam.

"Zombies?" Smudge's voice echoed in Sam's mind as soon as he appeared.

Pushing aside the shock at having the cat pop into his peripheral vision, Sam spoke. "An infestation," he said out loud. "In the school basement."

"Mal's school," Bob said pointedly.

"Can I see the book?" Smudge asked Sam.

Sam nodded, and, just as quickly, realized no one else could hear Smudge. "The book, Bob. Smudge wants to see the book."

Bob laid it on the ground next to the familiar and stepped back. Smudge appeared to consider the small square, then hissed at it. *"As I suspected, nothing in there can help us."* Then he did something Sam hadn't been expecting. With the curl of a clawed paw, he flicked the book into Sam's lap. Ms. Triplewine screamed, Bob yelled, and Sam braced himself for the worst.

Silence. Nothing happened. Sam wasn't erased from existence, or even worse, turned into a toad or a bloody pile of flesh.

Bob scooped the book away and threw it out of Sam's reach.

"Humans can't touch that!" Ms. Triplewine shrieked again. "Are you okay, Mr Enderson?" Sam could only stare at Smudge, who stared right back at him, a smug feline expression in his little cat face.

"Told you so," Smudge thought with a twitch of a tail. *"Not entirely human, are you?"*

"I'm going to feed you dog food," Sam snapped. There weren't a lot of ways Sam could threaten the familiar.

"You won't," Smudge replied mentally. *"Not when you realize I know how to clear the infestation."*

Sam waited expectantly and then, with a huff, finally asked out loud: "So what *is* the answer?" His familiar was a freaking drama king.

"It's simple. All we need is an avenging angel."

"An angel. Like an angel from heaven, that kind of an angel?"

"An angel? He says we need an angel? No one can contact an angel. Stupid cat," Bob muttered, glaring at the feline.

Smudge met Bob's eyes and very deliberately paused to scrape his claws on the floor.

"I have an angel who I can call in for favors. Wait here."

Chapter Two

NICK KLAUSON PUSHED OPEN THE DOOR TO THE TAVERN AND climbed onto a seat in the back corner, where it was dark and he could be alone. He needed somewhere to lick his wounds and this place was as good as any. The barman—woman? Nick could never tell with satyrs—waited expectantly, and Nick didn't keep him or her standing there long. He knew what he wanted and didn't have to think about what he was going to order.

"Whiskey. A bottle. One glass," he said firmly. He waited for a reaction and was vaguely disappointed when there was none. The whiskey was old, the crystal tumbler bright, and there, in front of him, was the means to forget who he was for a few hours at least.

"Do you want any food?" the satyr asked. Her features coalesced into a feminine shape, and she batted her eyelashes at Nick. If she only knew how freaked out Nick was to see another paranormal being able to change sex at the whim of the person they were with…

"Do I look like I want food?" Nick snapped. "If I'd wanted food…" He stopped as he realized the residual anger from his last showdown with the family was spilling over into spite and irritation. "Sorry," he mumbled. Swallowing another mouthful of burning alcohol, he wiped his mouth. "Bad day." *Bad year... bad life...*

The satyr leaned over the bar, giving Nick an eyeful of newly fashioned creamy breasts in a low cut top. "You look stressed," she began with a low purr. "I can help you with that if you have the time." Evidently, the satyr was reading Nick all wrong. The alcohol was burning in his system and he clung to the buzz as long as he could. Unfortunately, his family had this damn gene that meant they didn't stay drunk for long. Sometimes he hated that... sometimes he wanted to drown in the haze of contentment and just stay there for an hour or two.

"Wrong... uhm..." He waved a hand at her breasts.

She chuckled and in the weirdest, unsexiest, most obscene way ever, she morphed into a male. Nick nearly choked on his whiskey. The male bartender was *so* the absolute opposite of what Nick wanted in a guy. She... or he—or whatever the satyr was—had chosen a small blond twink of a thing. What he was faced with couldn't have been more wrong. Nick loved his men big, and dark-haired, and strong enough to drag him to bed.

"Better?" the satyr said in a soft voice.

Nope. All wrong.

"I'm not interested," Nick said quickly. "That isn't what I came in for."

The satyr reached out a hand and touched his cheek, startling him back on the stool. "Shame. You're soooo pretty."

Nick pulled away from the satyr's reach. "Uh. Yeah. Just the whiskey, thanks."

"Are you really sure? I can be anything you want me to be."

"Can you be a way out?" Nick snapped, then regretted it. The satyr eyed him with confusion, then opened his mouth to answer. "Never mind," Nick interjected. "The whiskey is fine."

The satyr moved away and morphed as he walked, back into the buxom blonde. Nick could feel the disappointment emanating from there. He hated that. Not only was Nick the only skinny one in the family, but he had a broken form of the family trait of empathy. Not a useful skill when the only emotions he was capable of reading were misery and disappointment. He couldn't even get empathy right. And as for ho ho *freaking* ho…

"Is this seat taken?" a voice rumbled to his left. Irritation flooded Nick. This was a big bar with a lot of spaces to hide, why would someone want to share his?

"Yes," he snapped.

The owner of the voice chuckled and the sound cut through Nick's melancholy. That was one low, sexy noise. He looked sideways and got an eyeful of man. Big man. Huge. Maybe six-four to his five-ten. Wide, solid, with dark hair, and even in the dim lighting at this end, Nick could see the man's eyes glinted with amusement. Nick squirmed in his seat. Why had he said yes? The man, or whatever he turned out to be in this mixed human/para bar, was clearly interested enough to choose to sit next to Nick. Add to that Nick had a whole afternoon to kill.

"No," he said.

"No what?" the big man said.

"When I said yes, I meant no. No one is sitting there."

The man looked down pointedly at the fact he was

already perched on the stool anyway. "Then I'll stay," he concluded.

The satyr behind the bar moved over to serve the new guy. Nick blinked furiously. The alcohol had clearly got to him because he could swear the satyr was morphing from male to female and was at times stuck as a bearded sixty-year-old man with the biggest chest he'd ever seen. He shook his head and concentrated on his whiskey. He was obviously losing it big-time.

"Zeph Constantine." The big man introduced himself and held out a hand to shake.

"Nick Klauson."

They shook hands and Nick winced at Zeph's grip. Firm, maybe a little too firm. The shaking went on for some time. Neither man released his hold. Finally, Nick realized he was still holding Zeph's hand, and embarrassment flushed his face. Thank the heavens they were in the gloom so Zeph didn't see the telltale signs of Nick's classic awkwardness around hot men.

"What brings you to the city?" Zeph asked as he sipped on what looked like water but could well have been vodka for all Nick knew.

"Toy convention," Nick answered immediately. Then his mind went blank. What else could he add to that one? That was his cover story, and he hadn't spent any time embellishing it to be able to give details.

"Interesting. And?" Zeph prompted.

"I'm a statistician," Nick lied on the run. "I look at trends in toy sales to support company marketing." So it wasn't actually lying, but he had fudged a little there. His actual job was to visit toy fairs and determine trends. But he was also there to investigate areas with any pockets of residual despair—the parts of the city and the surrounding countryside where there was a lack of joy. Not that he would tell sexy here anything about what he really did. His job description was a little screwy, but that was what he did and he did it well.

After all, he might not be able to sense joy, but he could certainly sense the absence of joy. There were spots of dark when he looked at a map where sadness was prevalent, hence the stop at this particular bar just off Quarter Street. He'd just cleared up one problem two roads over and thought he'd dealt with them all, only to see another at a school outside of the city. Schools should be happy places this close to Christmas and that could only mean trouble. That school was his first stop tomorrow on his way home.

Nick regarded going home with anticipation and dread. He loved his family, but that didn't stop him from being the black sheep. Although they tried to help by giving Nick work where he could use his abilities, he was always aware of their lingering disappointment over his lack of traditional skills.

"Interesting job," Zeph summarized.

"What is it you do?" Nick asked. *Fair's fair*—he wanted to know what this gorgeous guy did that allowed him to be in a bar at this moment, sitting this close to Nick and causing Nick's cock to sit up and take notice.

"This and that," Zeph said vaguely. "I'm in private law enforcement."

"Like a PI?"

Zeph nodded. "Yeah, something like that."

Nick cast a furtive look around them. "Are you here on a job at the moment?" he whispered.

Zeph smiled and shook his head. "In between jobs—just came to check in on my cousin, but he's not home. Thought I'd stick around and do some exploring. Ended up going past the door to this place and knew I had to come in for a drink.

Then, as luck would have it, I found a gorgeous, sexy, blond guy with pouty lips and come-to-bed eyes to sit next to."

Nick leaned around Zeph. "Where?" he asked, bemused. Then it hit him what Zeph had meant and again with the blushing. "You mean me?"

Zeph copied his action and looked around the bar before returning his gaze to Nick. "I don't see anyone else in here fitting that description."

"It's not blond," Nick hastened to point out. "My hair, that is. It's actually white."

Zeph peered closer. "So it is. How intriguing. And your eyes are a stunning icy blue."

Nick didn't think to comment that he was sure Zeph couldn't see his eye color in the gloom and instead focused on the fact that Zeph had used the word stunning. He wasn't anywhere near that level. He couldn't seem to put on weight if he tried. His hair was white, but had strands of blue in it that he had to keep pulling out, and his voice was soft and not at all gruff and deep like a proper Klauson. What was stunning about a slim, fair, normal guy?

"What color are your eyes?" Nick finally asked.

Zeph smiled. "Normal, ordinary green."

Nick doubted there was anything ordinary about Zeph, but he didn't say anything. He couldn't recall the last time he'd been picked up in a bar, and he'd never picked up someone himself. He wasn't even entirely sure what the etiquette of it was.

"So..." Nick needed a whole sentence that sounded clever. "What kind of cases do you work on? Cop type stuff? Or—"

"Yeah, like that." Zeph turned in his seat. "Listen, you want to get out of here?"

"I'm not... I don't... I have to..." Damn it. What did he

really want? To find the area of black now, or maybe spend some lip time with tall, dark, and sexy. "Yes," he finally said. Throwing bills down on the counter, he stood and hitched his jeans, which never quite sat right on his hips, and waited expectantly.

Very deliberately, Zeph stood and held out his hand, which Nick took. There was a light illuminating Zeph, and Nick saw his eyes… They were green as Zeph had said… but they were like emerald glass and held desire and promise in them. There was nothing ordinary about them at all. He stumbled after Zeph in a daze. He wasn't even sure what direction they were going until the noise of a fire door banging against a wall and the influx of daylight brought him back to the here and now. In reflex, he tugged at Zeph's hand, but he stopped immediately when Zeph spoke in reassurance.

"Everything is fine," he said gently.

How could everything be fine? He had just left a bar with a stranger who gripped his hand so tight it nearly hurt.

"But I—I don't do—do this," Nick stammered. He was suddenly a little scared and pulled his hand again.

"Do what?" Zeph asked and released his grip. He took a step backward and leaned against the wall.

"Fuck random strangers against walls by trash bins," Nick said. He rubbed at his hand and caught Zeph looking down at the hand and frowning. They stared at each other, and out here, in the daylight, Zeph looked harder and bigger and even more beautiful than Nick had thought. His raven black hair had loosened from whatever was holding the mass from around his face and his eyes weren't just emerald green— they held flecks of amber gold.

"I don't know my own strength." Zeph pointed at Nick's hand. "I'm sorry."

Nick hesitated to say that he was the kind of guy who

quite liked being manhandled—he didn't really want to give Zeph open season on him just yet.

"It's okay. Look, I don't do casual sex like this," Nick finished his thoughts.

Sadness flickered over Zeph's face. "Oh. But I wasn't looking for sex. You have very pretty lips—I just wanted a kiss."

Nick was confused. "But you said you wanted to leave. We could have kissed inside."

Zeph shuddered. "That satyr was staring at me."

"Who wouldn't?" Nick muttered. Zeph was physically perfect, an Adonis carved in flesh and blood—muscled and slim hipped with perfect features—a strong chin and a perfect nose, and as for his hair…

Zeph sighed and moved from the wall, pacing the small area away from Nick and back again. Nick felt dizzy. When Zeph was near to him, all his focus was on the beautiful man. But as soon as he walked away, the air of despair that always collected in the back alleys of the city began to wash over him. Seemed as if Zeph had a power of his own, exuding goodness and light and all that kind of stuff that the rest of Nick's family had in spades. That began to change subtly the more Zeph paced. Suddenly, despair was clear in the air around them, and Nick crossed his arms over his chest. It could be a combination of what had happened before, a residual touch of the need for connection between random strangers, but inside he knew it came from Zeph.

"All I wanted was a kiss," Zeph said sadly. He shrugged as he spoke and stopped in front of Nick with a forlorn expression on his face. "I know I did it all wrong. But I saw you and something inside me said I should talk to you. But I scared you."

"I'd like the kiss, and to talk," Nick offered.

Nick watched the play of emotions on Zeph's face, from sadness to hope, and he couldn't have been happier when the air of despair vanished from the man. Then Zeph grinned wickedly and his eyes crinkled at the corners.

"What?" Nick asked, suspicious.

Zeph crowded Nick against the wall and kissed him briefly and firmly. Nick sighed into the quick kiss, and went up on tiptoes to place a targeted kiss to Zeph's full lips. "More kisses," he said and smirked as he heard himself say the words.

Zeph cradled Nick's face deepening the kiss until they were pressed against the wall grinding against each other. Nick groaned into the kiss and closed his eyes. Then he collapsed in a heap on the ground. Opening his eyes, he realized Zeph had disappeared. Gone. Vanished. Nick stood and dusted himself off, glanced up and down the alley and even opened the bar exit to look inside.

Seriously? What the hell? Was his kissing that bad that Zeph had decided to just leave?

Great. Just fucking great.

Chalk another one up to the skinny guy's run of bad luck.

Chapter Three

ZEPH GLARED AT THE GROUP OF PEOPLE SURROUNDING HIM.
"What just happened?"

Smudge, his black cat familiar sidled up to him. "*You
need to help Sam.*"

"I was in the middle of something," Zeph growled. Damn
he'd almost had that cute guy in his grasp. Now Nick
probably thought Zeph deserted him. Damn. Zeph couldn't
remember the last time he had any action. He'd wanted to
take Nick to a hotel and check to see if his hair matched down
below.

Now he would never get another kiss.

He evaluated the group before him and came up at a loss.
"Why am I here?"

"We have a zombie problem."

Zeph turned his attention to the blond talking. His
handsome face had a sickly tinge as if he might throw up at
any moment.

"What's wrong with him?"

A vampire stepped in front of the blond. "Sam's finding
that zombies make him nauseous."

"Ah, an empath, huh?" Zeph had met a few in the past. They tended to be weak and not good for much.

"Not by birth," the vampire said vaguely.

"Smudge told us angels are good with dealing with zombies," Sam said, coughing.

"Depends."

"Depends on what?" Sam asked.

"Who are you people?"

The familiar sat in front of Zeph and flicked his tail; gold eyes narrowed menacingly. *"You'd best watch your manners, angel, or I can send you to visit with your cousins."*

Zeph stepped back. "Understood. I'm Zeph Constantine, how can I help you?"

Everyone knew not to mess with a familiar, especially when they had a task in mind.

"I'm Sam Enderson and this is my partner Bob," the blond offered.

"Soul mate, not partner," the vampire corrected.

Zeph smiled when Sam rolled his eyes.

"I'm not going around telling everyone that you're my soul mate."

Bob scowled. "Why not?"

"Because it sounds weird. I refuse to sound like I'm starring in a romance novel."

"I'm Zeph Constantine." He held out his hand to shake. "Nice to meet you both."

A zap went through Zeph when they shook hands.

"Wow," Sam said.

Zeph stepped away from Sam. "I thought you were human."

Sam made a growling sound.

"We don't talk about that," the vampire said.

Zeph decided his questions could wait. He didn't want to

be on the wrong side of the humanlike blond. "Zombies, you say?"

"The school's basement is filled with zombies," Sam said. "Why?"

"What do you mean why?" Bob asked.

"Why are there zombies?" Zeph asked. "Is the basement filled with dead bodies?"

A woman stepped forward. She had the air of someone who considered herself to be important.

"I'm Ms. Triplewine, headmistress of this school."

Zeph nodded, not offering his hand. His fingers still tingled from touching the supposed human.

"Nice to meet you. Is there a reason your school is filled with dead bodies, Ms. Triplewine?"

The headmistress's mouth tightened to almost a flat line before she finally answered. "The school was short of funds when this structure was built. To get a good deal on land we had to build over an old cemetery."

"What is this, a horror movie?" Sam asked in a shocked tone.

"Don't be a prude, young man," the headmistress scolded. "No one wanted to claim the bodies. It's not like we covered someone's loved ones. All the cemetery held were old bones no one wanted anymore. In fact, we made certain no one wanted to claim the bodies before we began construction. We even placed magical protection on the grounds to keep them from rising again."

Zeph let out a long breath. "Apparently, the wards have broken down, or they wouldn't be up and around. Where are the kids?" He spotted one girl sitting on the steps, watching them with interest, but no others were around.

"Most of them are on holiday break, visiting with their parents. We have a handful that stay all year round for various reasons. We've moved them to the rooms over the chapel. It's hallowed ground so they'll be safe there," the headmistress said in short, staccato words, as if she hated to spare a single syllable to explain herself to anyone.

"Do we know what raised them?" Zombies didn't just pop out of nowhere. Someone had to trigger their need.

Sam cleared his throat. "There's a necromancer causing problems right now. We believe he raised them to distract us."

"From what?"

"We're not sure," Bob said. "We believe this same necromancer had the dragon king murdered and tried to make another dragon shifter his puppet. We think he's trying to take control over the supernatural world a little bit at a time."

"It will take more than a handful of zombies to take over the world," Zeph argued. He hated the thought of a necromancer running loose. He had never met a necromancer who did anything positive.

"We think he's on a multiple step process. We prevented him from taking over the dragon shifters so it could be that he's trying another tactic," Sam explained. "Bob can take you to the zombies. They make me sick to my stomach."

Zeph nodded. As much as he wanted to stay and interrogate Sam to find out what he really was, they needed to solve the zombie problem.

The school oozed with magic. So much magic had been practiced within these walls, it probably took the necromancer limited effort to collect the power that had soaked into the building and turn it to his advantage. Zeph hated to think what would happen if there hadn't been any hallowed ground. The cemetery they'd built the school on had to be extremely old not to have been blessed before the bodies were buried.

He watched as Bob kissed Sam with a thoroughness that had more to do with claiming than anything else.

Zeph waited until they'd walked away from the others before he spoke. "I'm not after your man, Bob."

Bob laughed, a sound that held little true amusement. "Trust me, everyone wants Sam. Once you've been near him long enough, you'll want him too. His appeal grows on you. At least, it does on every other damn person on the planet." Bob growled as if revisiting a particularly annoying memory.

Remembering the jolt of energy that had traveled from Sam's hand to his, Zeph had to ask, "I know you said you don't like to talk about it, but what exactly is he?"

"He's a bit of everything. A sort of mishmash of paranormals. Sam still likes to think of himself as human, though."

"Why?" Zeph thought having a bunch of para blood and capabilities was far superior to being human.

"He has a bit of a hang-up over paras."

"He didn't seem to have a problem with you."

Bob gave him a wide, satisfied smile. "I've been working on him for a while now."

"Hmm." Zeph didn't say anything more. They'd reached the door to the basement, and the overwhelming despair hit him like a body blow. "How many are there down there?"

Bob shrugged. "A lot. We didn't get a very good look before Sam became sick. Ms. Triplewine is in denial. She seems to believe they'll be easily eradicated. I'm thinking if they're really old, it might be harder to persuade them to go back into the earth."

"You're right. It's always the older ones who fight it the most. It generally takes more magic to raise them, since their spirit has left them, which also makes it harder to put them back down."

"Good luck with this lot then." Bob waved a hand toward the door for Zeph to go ahead.

"You're not going in with me?"

Bob laughed. "If I take one step in that room, Sam will know and I'm more concerned over Sam's anger than a bunch of zombies. If you need help, yell."

"I can see who wears the pants in your relationship—your little non-human."

"Maybe, but he's more persuasive when he's not wearing anything at all." With that parting shot, Bob walked away.

Zeph took a deep breath and gathered a pool of magic in his gut. From a sheath between his wings, he pulled out his blessed sword. "It's time to kill some zombies."

Chapter Four

NICK SAT AT THE BAR, CONTINUING TO DRINK FOR A BIT. THE whiskey had vanished along with the hot guy so Nick moved on to the hard stuff.

Nick slugged back his drink. He couldn't believe Zeph just dumped him like that. Well, actually he could. It was right on par with the rest of his life right then. Magic sucks, check. Job sucks, check. First hot man he'd seen in a while vanishes without a trace. Yep, everything was right on track for his sucktacular life.

Depressed, he slouched down on his bar stool and motioned to the bartender. "Give me another."

"I don't think you can handle any more peppermint cocoa, hon," the satyr said. "The sugar alone could kill you."

"Trust me. My family has a complete immunity to sugar." At least that was one trait he shared with the others.

"If you're sure, but if you puke on my floor, you're cleaning it."

Nick didn't answer—he just waved for another drink. The longer he sat there, the more a nagging sensation tugged at his brain, as if he'd forgotten to do something.

Closing his eyes, Nick focused on the feeling.

Dread. Thick, cloying, despair. Nick pulled out his map and slapped it on the bar. Scanning the neighborhoods, it took him a moment to pinpoint the source.

"There." He stabbed a finger at the school he'd planned to visit tomorrow. The emotions slamming into him told Nick it would be too late if he waited. He'd better investigate it tonight.

"Here you go." The satyr set a cup of peppermint cocoa before him.

Nick tossed back the hot beverage, then left some money on the bar, more than enough to cover his costs.

"You need anything else?"

Nick wiped his mouth with his sleeve. "I need a lot of stuff, but unless you've got a pocketful of wishes, I think you've done all you can." He added a bit more for a tip and headed for the door.

Unfortunately without his uncle's sled, he'd have to travel the old-fashioned way—by taxi.

TWENTY MINUTES LATER, the cab dropped Nick off at the gates to the school. He caught a glimpse of the building through the trees and shuddered—so gloomy. He figured it probably didn't have such a depressing look normally, but the horrible despair pouring from the place didn't help put it in a happy light.

Taking a deep breath, Nick opened the gate and walked up the driveway. The driver wouldn't go any closer, and to be fair, Nick couldn't blame the guy.

Approaching the gothic building, Nick admired the flower boxes overflowing with bright colored blooms and the neatly tended path. He imagined they were there to soften the otherwise dramatic stonework. Gargoyles sat at each corner and somehow every single one of them was looking down at him as he approached. Then he noticed something else—it was deadly silent. There were no birds or bees or any sign of life, and it sent a chill down his spine. Something unnatural lurked inside the school, and it was Nick's job to figure out how to fix it before Christmas. If he didn't take care of the problem before his Uncle Claus flew his reindeer over the town, Nick would be in even more trouble than usual.

He took a step closer, and his misery sensors tingled. Something wasn't right here. He could feel the despair, but it was deadened, muffled. He swore he could hear shouting, raised voices, and even screaming, but he couldn't pinpoint the source. There had to be some serious magic at work if he couldn't see what should be right in front of his eyes, yet still see the school. He stopped and listened.

"Where's Mal?"

"Has anyone seen Mal?"

"Why did you let her go down there?"

Tentatively he stepped forward and his ears popped as he pushed through an invisible barrier to arrive in a scene of chaos. A tall vampire was holding back a blond human. The despair emanating from them both was excruciatingly painful. Nick pressed his hands over his ears to cut out the shouting and instead cataloged everything he could see. He found two people fighting over someone called Mal and an older woman, in a tweed suit and pearls, agitated and terrified. About twenty kids were peering through the windows above the gallery.

Nick rolled his head and stretched his neck. The tension was so thick in there he could slice through it with his blade. No one had noticed him yet. He circled back and around to the children in the chapel. The terror in their faces was almost too much to bear, but the despair that emanated from the school hadn't quite touched them.

Deciding they were safe for now, Nick spun on his heel, then pulled his knife from his jacket and strode toward the arguing men. As he grew closer, the scent and taste of desolation was near overwhelming. It wasn't from the vampire and the human, but from something else. Something evil. Gripping his blade, he stopped next to the vampire.

"Tell me," was all he said. He might be a misfit in the family, but he was well trained with the instincts of many generations ingrained into him—he knew his job and he knew it well. The vampire glanced at him, and the human in his grip took the opportunity to dart by him and disappear through an oak door. The vampire shoved Nick out of the way and followed the human. Nick went to follow, but the wall of evil that blocked his way was nearly impenetrable. He whispered the only magic he had control of, then, utterly determined, he pushed his way inside.

The doorway led into a dark corridor, and at the end of it, spiral stairs that went down and down, beyond basement level, under the school. Finally, it opened to a wide cavern ringed with a viewing balcony of sorts. The dark was all-consuming, but he thought he saw a glimpse of a white shirt and followed the image. The magic he had pulled from inside him was dwindling—he was like a phone constantly losing his charge—and he stumbled against the metal railings that stopped him from falling into the nothing below.

The moaning and screaming on the other side of the walkway was terrible, a cacophony of grating sounds that made him unable to think properly. He stumbled again, but this time there was a reason for it. The vampire was on his knees over a prone figure—the human.

"Are you okay?" he shouted over the noise of the wailing and moaning.

"Sam's down!" the vampire shouted. "I have to get him out. I can't find Mal."

Nick crouched and assisted the vampire in picking up the human called Sam. A spark of light brightened the walkway as he touched Sam, and he shook his hand at the static electricity in the touch. The vampire steadied himself and heaved Sam into his arms.

"I'll be back," he said strongly.

Nick instantly disagreed. "You can't be in here," he said loudly. "You have to stay outside. Let me handle this."

The vampire shook his head. "I have to find Mal."

"Who's Mal?"

"Our daughter."

"You take him out. I'll find Mal."

The vampire looked torn.

"This is my job," Nick snapped. "Do what I say."

"But Mal is in there."

"I'll find Mal. Take your man outside."

Bob turned to leave, then turned abruptly. "Mal is a vampire child," he called back.

Nick waved a hand to indicate he had heard. Taking the few seconds he needed, he strengthened his magical shield to protect himself. Hell knew how long this would last—he'd never encountered such a dark spot. A flash of white startled him and he pressed himself flat against the wall. An explosion burst just above his head, making the rock shift beneath his fingers. Fuck. What was down there?

Cautiously, but with as much speed as he could manage while not falling on his face, he reached another set of stairs. Peering into the black, he imagined he was face to face with a sea of bodies, moving and swaying and reaching for him.

"Shit. Zombies."

He'd only ever read about them in the history books his uncle made him study. The great zombie infestation of 'Twenty-Three was the very last time one of his family had died going up against a target. Steeling himself, he tightened his grip on his blade. In one smooth motion, he passed the blade directly into the heart of the nearest zombie—a tall emaciated man with yellow teeth and no hair. The sight was disgusting. No person alive should have to put eyes on the dead. As he expected, as soon as the blade passed through the zombie's heart, it vanished in a mist. For a second, Nick could see nothing beyond that mist. He couldn't see even the next zombie, much less focus in on its heart. Stabbing at any zombie he saw, the elvish blade passed through them and the mist grew deeper. He couldn't see the vampire child and had no sense of her being anywhere near him. He knew what he was wading through—the residue of the dark magic that had called the dead to life. He held his breath as he attempted to wait for the mist to clear, but it lingered and twisted around him, and not for the first time he wished one of his cousins was there fighting with him.

Hands gripped him. He chopped and hacked himself free, ignoring the screams of pain and the moaning. A sea of hands reached for him in endless waves. He could feel his magical protection beginning to fail against the ferocity of the anguish and blackness being forced at him. Another flash of white and this time it carved a great gash into the soil and stone and exposed a seam of quartz. Nick ducked and tried to see where this was coming from. The dark was all-consuming, and he couldn't see shit.

The waves of zombies lessened, and he took the time to consider what to do next. The mist had dissipated a little, and he could see a little beyond the group struggling at the bottom of the stairs, as his eyes grew more accustomed. There was a gap there, and the rest of them—mouths wide and desperate for food—had someone caught in the center of them. Without thought, he forced himself through the group, and stood back-to-back with whoever was dealing with sending the dead back to sleep. If the other person felt him there, he said nothing as they hacked and carved.

He heard a call for help.

"I've got this!" he shouted. He tripped his way in the dark until he could see where a small child was hanging from a root about eight feet up in the air; a group of zombies were clawing and climbing to reach her.

"Don't let go!" he shouted near uselessly. A few moves and the zombies that had her surrounded became nothing but dust. He held up his hands. "Jump!" he ordered. She didn't cry, she didn't argue—she simply dropped into his arms. He grabbed her close and, without another glance, made his way through the darkness, as best as he could remember, to the stairs. He looked down at the tall figure of a man facing away from him and at the glow of white that surrounded him.

"We're done!" Nick shouted. "Let's go."

The man waved a blade and stepped into darkness.

"I need to finish this…"

The words echoed in his head like they had been shouted to all, but Nick could swear they were in his head and spoken personally to him.

"Are you Mal?" he asked the small girl in his arms.

She nodded and buried her face in his neck. Suddenly, he was torn. His duty was to the child. Hell, his whole reason for being was to protect children—he knew that—but could he leave whoever was fighting and disappear from here?

A stray zombie passed them and Mal yelped. One swift move of his blade and Nick dispatched the zombie—but as it did, Nick felt pain. Seemed like the last of his magic was leaving the premises. He would be just another man without his defenses.

He held Mal close and sprinted as fast as he could up the stairs, around the balcony area, and up through the corridors until finally he burst out into the blessedly cool air.

He dropped Mal carefully, with a quiet prayer to whoever was listening, he turned to go back inside. The door slammed shut on him, stopping him from getting in. He pushed and shoved at it, but it was not budging. Helplessly, he faced the vampire and the human, and little Mal.

"Why did you go in there?" the human asked desperately of her.

"I wanted to see," Mal hiccupped between sobs.

"Don't ever do that again," the vampire added brokenly. "We love you and if anything happened to you…"

Nick interrupted the touching scene. "I need to get back in," he said. "Please help me."

The vampire gave Mal one last hug and joined him at the door. Together, they pushed, but it didn't move. They left the door, and Nick shook his head.

"He's still down there. I don't know who he is, but I have to help him."

The human came over at that point with Mal in his arms.

"He's an angel," Sam offered gently. "My familiar called him. He's the only one who can clear the zombies."

Not the only one, Nick thought, though he didn't say anything. Nick could clear them—he just couldn't settle their souls like an angel could. The angel had shut the door—locked Nick out in an attempt to… do what? Save Nick? Protect him? Nick slumped to the floor and leaned back against the stone wall.

The vampire crouched in front of him. "I'm Bob and this

is Sam," he said, indicating the human as he held out his hand. "Thank you," he added.

Nick shook the proffered hand. "No problem. How is Sam?"

Bob closed his eyes briefly and grief carved his features. "I can't lose him," he said brokenly. "If you hadn't come down there—"

"He's fine now," Nick interrupted. "He's safe."

"I don't know how to thank you—"

"I'm Nick by the way."

Nick hated the emotion filled *thank-you*s. His cousins said that the gratitude and happiness were the greatest high they'd ever had. The only positive thing he ever felt was the absence of evil and despair—not exactly a high.

The door crashed open, and a figure strode out. Big and menacing, and with the shadows of wings about his head, he held a long sword that glowed with white light.

Nick blinked and looked again. There was something familiar in the way the man held himself, in the way he stood proud and huge and certain.

Zeph? Could it be? Was it…?

The light lowered in brightness then vanished altogether and finally a man stood there, exhausted but whole. It was Zeph. Shit. Zeph from the bar was an angel?

Nick had been kissed by an angel?

Chapter Five

Zeph stared at Nick for a moment. His mouth dried up at the sight of the man from the bar. Even after fighting zombies, the flavor of Nick's mouth still haunted him. He licked his lips. When Nick's eyes followed the motion, he knew he was doomed.

"What are you doing here, Nick?"

Nick's mouth dropped open. "What am *I* doing here? I noticed you left out a little detail when we talked earlier."

Zeph crossed his arms over his chest. He refused to back down. "Yeah? I don't remember you saying anything about fighting zombies as a side hobby when we talked earlier either."

Nick stepped forward. He lifted his hand and slid a finger along Zeph's back where his wings had retreated. "I also don't remember you saying anything about being an angel. I'm sure that would've stuck in my head even though you're an amazing kisser."

Zeph stepped closer until their chests brushed together. He sucked in a breath at the immediate sizzle of attraction that zapped between them. Damn, Nick pushed all his sexual attraction buttons.

"Do you have a problem with angels?"

"Um, no. I have a problem with guys who vanish and leave me wanting."

Zeph cupped Nick's face between his hands. "I didn't want to go. I was summoned by Sam's familiar. I owed him a favor, and he decided to call it in."

Nick's anger faltered. "I guess I can't hold that against you. Did you get all the zombies?"

"No. I mean, I got those, but I can feel others nearby. I don't know what kind of necromancer is on the loose, but he's really powerful. I think I'll need to stick around in case others rise. You never did say why you were here."

Nick bit his lip.

Zeph cupped Nick's shoulders. "Whatever it is, hon, it can't be that bad. It's not like you were hiding wings."

Nick laughed as Zeph had hoped he would.

"No. I'm not keeping any wings from you. I'm a Klauson."

"A what?"

"My uncle is Santa Claus. I'm half elf."

Zeph opened his mouth to speak, then snapped it shut again. "I've heard of the Klauson family; bringers of light and laughter." He narrowed his eyes. "You don't look like a Klauson."

Nick snorted. "Yeah, I get that a lot when people find out. I don't have the padding the rest of my cousins do." Nick patted his flat stomach. "And I can't grow a beard to save my life."

"So the toy convention story is a cover."

"Not entirely. Sometimes I go to toy conventions. Got to keep up with the latest trends, you know."

Zeph cleared his throat and tried to get his brain back on track. He'd expected a lot of explanation—but not that one. "I didn't realize that the Klauson family fights zombies."

Nick sighed and rolled his eyes. "We don't publicize it. We can sense dark pockets in the world. Places where despair has taken root and is oppressing the people. My job is to eradicate them so Santa has a smooth trip on Christmas Eve."

"Seriously?"

"What, you didn't think he just sashayed across the world in one night without running into any problems, did you? I can't have him hopping down a chimney and running into a zombie or a necromancer. If I can't eradicate the darkness, I have to mark it on his map as a place to avoid. I came to the school because we shouldn't have an entire school marked off his list without a good reason."

"I thought you guys were all about making toys and giving out candy canes." Zeph resolved to take a visit to the para-library to research the Klauson family in more detail.

"Yeah, well, it's not all tinsel and sugar cookies. If we've finished here, I'm gonna go."

"Wait!" Zeph didn't know why, but he didn't want Nick to leave.

Nick raised an eyebrow at him. "Why?"

Bob interrupted Zeph. "The necromancer still hasn't been caught. Any help would be appreciated. We're trying to figure out where he's hiding out and what his final goal is."

Zeph stared at the vampire. Here was the perfect opportunity to keep Nick by his side. "That's true. With all the children around, he'll be attracted to their innocence. It would be best if we stayed close to keep an eye on the school. I don't think all the activity is gone. A necromancer wouldn't be able to resist an entire school of paranormal kids, if only to drain them of their powers."

"You think he'd do that?" a pale-faced Sam asked.

"I'm not leaving the school," Mal declared. "I want to stay. Please, Sam."

Zeph could tell by the way the vampire stayed silent that Sam was the decision-maker in this group.

A heavy, expectant silence weighed in.

"Where's Ms. Triplewine?" Sam asked.

Everyone looked around, but the lady wasn't anywhere to be found.

"Surely she wouldn't have just left," Bob said.

Zeph closed his eyes and tried to focus on finding her trail.

Nothing.

"She must've been taken rather than walked away," Nick said, echoing Zeph's silent conclusion.

"What makes you think that?" Zeph asked, curious about Nick's reasoning.

"There's no psychic trail. I would think a woman who ran a magical school would have a bit of power," Nick replied.

"So we can't trace where she was taken to?" Sam asked with a resigned sigh.

Zeph shook his head and turned to Nick to see if he agreed.

"Even with the low reserves I have at the moment, I'm usually able to see the signatures of magic. Since there isn't any psychic signature in the air, it means she was snatched, probably teleported, out of this room."

"I see it's not your first time on a case. Nice evaluation," Zeph praised. Not only was Nick a good kisser, but apparently he also was a kick-ass magic user.

Nick blushed. "I don't have a lot of abilities, not like the other members of my family, but I can sense darkness."

"Don't knock your powers. That's a good one." Zeph

didn't like how Nick talked down about his skills. He'd killed quite a few zombies down in that basement. "I'd take you into battle with me anytime."

A higher compliment Zeph didn't have.

"Why don't you two come back to our place? We can discuss what we know about the necromancer there," Bob said.

Zeph looked at Nick. They both nodded. "That's a good idea. The quicker we resolve this, the faster I can move on to other things."

"I didn't realize we were holding you up." Nick's icy voice brought Zeph up short.

"No. I didn't mean that. I just need to go check in on my cousin and date this hot elf I met."

Nick laughed. "In that case, let's get going so we can move on to the fun things."

"Now we're on the same page." Zeph wrapped an arm around Nick's waist and followed the other couple out of the school. Zeph didn't generally assign emotions to buildings—that was too sentimental for him—but the stone building had a sense of sorrow as if it had draped itself in despair.

He shook off the feeling as he followed Sam, Bob, and Mal from the structure. "What about the other kids?" He pointed above only to see the line of children was now gone.

"Where did they go?" Nick asked.

"The teachers probably corralled them back to the other section of the school. They weren't supposed to be up there anyway," Bob said.

"Do you think we should go talk to them?" Sam asked. "They might have seen something."

"Excuse me?"

Zeph spun on his heel at the quiet voice behind them.

"Yes?" he replied quickly. The small gnome looked up at him from his three-foot height.

"I am Horace Horryville, deputy head. The children are understandably upset at hearing about the infestation and seeing our beloved headmistress disappear in front of their eyes," the gnome said softly. "We'd quite like it if you could allow us the time to settle them. Already two of our children are in with the matron, suffering from acute hives."

"Did you see her disappear?" Sam asked firmly.

"I did," the gnome answered with a nod. "Just vanished into thin air—we saw nothing else."

"That isn't good," Nick muttered.

"We're taking Mal home with us," Sam said.

"No," Mal contradicted. "Sam, I want to stay here with my friends."

Zeph watched as Sam went to his knees in front of the little vampire child. Bob joined him, and they hugged and whispered between the three of them. Finally, Bob stood and helped Sam to his feet. Evidently, agreement had been reached and Mal went and stood by Horace.

"We should come back tomorrow," Zeph said softly to the group around him.

Horace grasped Mal's hand and the two of them disappeared through the front door. Bob took an instinctive step to follow, but Zeph was surprised to see that this time it was Sam stopping Bob. Those two loved that little girl—she was very lucky for their unconditional love.

"I don't know about the rest of you, but I'm tired," Bob replied, not giving anyone else a chance to speak. Zeph could see the vampire was staring right at Sam, who looked exhausted. He imagined it wasn't that Bob was tired at all but Bob's need to get Sam somewhere horizontal for sleep.

"Agreed," Zeph said immediately. "We're not going to

find Ms. Triplewine any faster if we miss out on sleep. We can discuss strategy, recharge ourselves, then try again in the morning."

Zeph could see resistance in Sam's eyes, but the vampire made good sense. The kids weren't going anywhere, and even if they saw her get snatched, clearly they would have no idea where she had gone.

SAM'S NEED for sleep disappeared as he stared at the mess that used to be his office. *Have I been burgled?* Paperclips were scattered across the floor, a wire wastebasket had been toppled over, and a suspicious amount of squeaking was coming from under his couch.

"What's going on here?" he asked Smudge, the only resident he could see.

Smudge flicked his tail. *"You said you'd help me rescue other familiars."*

"Um, yeah." Sam searched the room, trying to spot whatever creature Smudge had brought into his office.

"There you have it. Your first project." Smudge sat in his pretty kitty pose, front paws perfectly aligned and his tail curled around his body.

"You're not going to distract me by pretending to be a cat. What did you bring here?" A sense of dread rolled through Sam. He just knew this wouldn't end well. He could tell by the pleased expression on Smudge's furry face.

"He's under the desk."

Sam stared at Smudge, but the cat familiar didn't give him any more clues. "It better not bite."

"I make no promises."

Sam went to his knees.

"What are you doing?" Bob asked from the doorway. "If I'm not in here, that position is completely wasted."

Sam shook his head. "Smudge brought me my first project. I'm trying to figure out what it is."

Bob took a deep breath. "Ferret."

"Really?" Sam glared at Smudge. "Aren't they rats or something?"

"They are part of the mustelid family," Bob said.

"What?"

"You know—otters, minks. Long, furry creatures."

"How do you know that?" Sam stared at his lover, wondering where this animal knowledge was coming from.

Bob shrugged. "When you live as long as I have, you pick up things."

"Do they bite?"

"Not usually very hard." Bob walked closer as if wanting in on the action.

"Great. Don't let me stop you from jumping in here," Sam said.

Bob held up his hands in defense. "Now don't get me involved. You're the one who made a deal with your familiar. I wouldn't dare interfere."

"Coward," Sam muttered. He crouched down to peek beneath his desk. A little whiskered nose poked out. It made chuffing, squeaking, snorting sounds.

"He's very vocal."

"He's trying to talk to you psychically. He doesn't realize you're mine." Smudge sauntered closer. A spark of magic ran across Sam. He could almost hear Smudge speaking telepathically to the ferret, but he couldn't quite make out the words.

After a moment, the small animal slid out from beneath Sam's desk and climbed up on Sam's knee.

"Well, hello there." Sam held up his fingers for sniffing.

The ferret obediently checked out Sam's hand. After several sniffs, the ferret sneezed. The desk levitated off the floor, then dropped back down again.

"What was that?" Sam asked, staring at his suddenly possessed desk.

"The ferret is named Pablo. He can move things with his mind. He is a minor familiar so he only has one ability. When he finds his owner, his skills will increase."

"Interesting." Sam had known Smudge was powerful but to learn of an entire classification of familiars brought new insight to Smudge's position on the familiar hierarchy.

"Smudge is one of the most powerful familiars I've ever met," Bob offered.

"Couldn't you have mentioned that before?" Sam asked.

Bob rolled his eyes. "Would it have mattered?"

"I guess not." Sam hated to agree, but since Smudge had chosen him, Sam hadn't exactly had a pick of familiars.

Sam picked up the ferret. Standing, he cradled the little creature in his arms. "So I need to find him a friend? That's it?"

"You have to find him the right friend."

"How am I supposed to do that?"

"That is your problem. Mine is to find you familiars that you can find homes for."

"Glad to hear I have a job. Not a paying one, but still a job." At this rate, he'd starve to death before he got a paying gig.

Bob laughed. "You aren't going to starve, love. I'll take care of you."

"Yeah, because I so want to become a kept man. How did you know that was my life goal?"

Bob rubbed his chin. "To do the job right, you might want

to invest in some tiny leather shorts and get your nipples pierced."

"I will end you, vampire," Sam threatened. He continued to pet the ferret. The small beast leaped out of his hands and jumped onto the couch where he proceeded to burrow himself between the cushions.

"Don't worry. He's a familiar, not a true animal. He won't get lost."

Sam had to go with Smudge's calm assessment, but he just knew his building was about to become a familiar petting zoo.

Bob kissed Sam on the forehead. "It'll be fine, love. Maybe you can charge admission."

Sam sighed. "Let's go talk to the angel and the elf. Crap. I never thought I'd say something like that and have it sound normal."

His life had taken a decidedly strange turn.

Chapter Six

NICK WAS HIDING. HE COULD FOOL HIMSELF THAT HE WAS using the bathroom, washing his hands, and it was taking time to do it all. But, if he was honest, he'd been in there fifteen minutes, and he was most definitely hiding. He'd driven back with Sam and Bob, but Zeph had extended ethereal wings and vanished in a silver mist. Freaking dramatic exit if Nick had ever seen one.

One more barrier between an angel and a half-elf.

As soon as Zeph appeared at the office door, Nick left. He excused himself, and now he was locked in the downstairs bathroom, standing in front of the mirror and flushing with embarrassment. He'd tried to be all confident badass in front of Zeph back at the school, but it hadn't worked. Yes, they'd fought and he'd proven his skills, but when communication needed to happen, he lost it. All that crackling, sparking attraction between them and Nick couldn't do a thing about getting his head around it.

"Nick? You okay?" Zeph said from outside the door.

"Out in a minute," Nick called immediately. Clutching the sink, he peered into the cracked and misted mirror. Horrified, he spotted a clump of blue hair in the white. A clump. Not a single hair but a whole shank of hair that went from root to tip in a wide stripe. Fuck. Something had happened in that battle, and he'd gone from being able to pass as a full Klauson to being quite obviously the freaky hybrid he was, overnight. He'd have to dye it because there was no way he was living with any visible signs of his human heritage. He was already pointed at enough at Klauson Inc. family meetings.

"Nick?" Zeph sounded worried.

"I'm fine," Nick snapped. Then he bent his head in despair. He had royally fucked up this entire thing. You don't just kiss an angel. There were rules. He must have missed the part where Zeph had admitted what he was so that Nick was given the chance to leave. Nick closed his eyes. Angels usually told you who they were. Then you knew where you stood with their unimaginable power. And you *certainly* didn't kiss them. He wracked his brains to recall the moment Zeph told him, but he couldn't remember a single word that sound like *"Hi, my name is Zeph and I am an angel."*

"I didn't tell you." The voice was much closer, and Nick let out an unmanly squeal of shock at the fact that, without having opened the door, Zeph now stood behind him. He pivoted on his heel and managed to stop himself from falling on his ass by grabbing at the sink behind him. Zeph was in the small room, large as life and twice as sexy. He had his arms crossed over his chest and an expression of remorse on his beautiful ethereal features. "I looked at you and I didn't want you to judge me before we'd connected."

"So I'm not going mad then," Nick said.

"No."

"You're supposed to warn people. It's the law."

"I know."

"So why didn't you?"

"Because…" Zeph uncrossed his arms and dug his hands into the pockets of his tailored black pants. The move drew Nick's glance to said pants and the prize that they hid. He swallowed back the desire in him. No angel would ever be with anything less than a pureblood of any paranormal, and even then, he'd never heard of elves or human beings on any pureblood list for angel liaisons.

Nick felt he should prompt Zeph. "Because…?"

Zeph let out a long sigh, and sadness filled his green eyes. "I don't know what made me walk in the bar," he began softly. "I just know that I could no more go past the door than I could blame my cousin Danjal for using brimstone."

Nick waited for Zeph to expand on that point, but he didn't. Instead, he took a step closer and crowded Nick against the sink.

"Nick, gorgeous, I knew my destiny was inside the door," Zeph announced dramatically.

"Destiny? Yours… mine… What?" Nick inhaled the scent of the angel just inches away from him and he was as hard as steel in seconds. Zeph was every fragrance that Nick loved— vanilla, chocolate, peppermint—and all Nick wanted to do was kiss him.

"When I saw you on the stool, I knew you were the one for me and all I wanted was a kiss to see if I was right. If I had told you who I was, what would you have done?"

The question threw Nick. He frowned. "Do? I'd have done what I was supposed to do. Angels don't kiss elves, especially half-elves."

"I didn't want you to refuse my kiss. That's why I didn't tell you." Zeph pressed himself against Nick, and Nick whimpered at his touch. He was so turned on listening to Zeph's voice as it rumbled around him.

"Zeph…" The name was a plea for more. More kissing, touching, feeling Zeph's hard body pushing him against a wall. Any wall.

"Do you believe in love at first sight?" Zeph asked. He punctuated the question with the softest of kisses to Nick's ear.

"Guh" was all Nick could manage in response. Zeph chuckled, and resting his hands on Nick's hips, he finally began to kiss Nick like he'd wanted. Soft, then harder, rougher, more, deeper… Nick lost himself in the kisses.

Banging on the door interrupted them after a while. "It's Bob. Is everything okay, Nick?"

Zeph moved back to allow Nick to talk. "I'm fine," Nick said hurriedly. He wanted more kissing, and he ignored the voice.

"Is Zeph in there with you?"

Nick looked up at Zeph—into emerald eyes wide with lust and need. "Uh-huh," he said.

"Zeph, Danjal is here. He says he knows you."

Zeph frowned and sighed. Pulling Nick close, he buried his face in Nick's neck before grabbing him and kissing him.

"I'll be there in five," he said. "Tell him to wait."

"'Kay." Bob's footsteps indicated he'd left the bathroom door.

"I don't want to stop," Zeph murmured. "I want to taste all of you."

"How did this Danjal know you were here?" Nick asked through the fog of desire. Then he forgot the question as Zeph released his hold and fell gracefully to his knees in front of Nick. In seconds, he had his pants open and his mouth on Nick, humming appreciatively around the length of him. He looked up at Nick who stared back; mesmerized at the fact his angel's eyes were now sparking with amber. There was no way he was going to last long, not when he could see the stretch of Zeph's gorgeous mouth around his cock. Zeph closed his eyes, and Nick whimpered at the loss of eye contact, but when Zeph concentrated his lips and tongue and tested the weight of Nick's balls with clever fingers, it was game over.

"Zeph… please… I'm coming…" He attempted to push Zeph away, but if anything, the angel sucked harder until, with a cry, Nick's orgasm had him shooting down Zeph's throat. Zeph stood and had his pants open in a second.

"Finish me," Zeph murmured into a kiss. "Please," he added.

Nick reached a hand in, wrapped his fingers around the angel's cock, and it was freaking perfect.

"So close," Zeph warned him, then deepened the kiss. Nick didn't have the correct angle for doing what he really needed to do. Somehow though, the grasp of his hand, plus the kissing, plus the magic of an orgasm from Nick, had Zeph coming. He keened and stiffened against Nick and lost it hot and hard in Nick's hand.

Breathing heavily, they stood immobile for the longest time.

"In answer to your question…" Nick began gently.

"Hmmm?" Zeph seemed kind of out of it—his green eyes heavy with emotion.

"I never believed in love at first sight… until I saw you." Zeph rested his forehead on Nick's and exhaled gently.

"Thank you," he said cryptically.

They kissed again, then hurried to get cleaned up and dressed.

"I like this," Zeph said as he carded a hand through Nick's hair. "It's new and it's beautiful."

Nick immediately clamped his hand over Zeph's and the

obvious blue stripe. "No, it's not," he snapped, irritated. "I'm going to dye it when I get home."

Zeph frowned. "Why would you do that?" he asked, puzzled. "It's part of you and I love it."

Nick wanted to say that Zeph's opinion counted for nothing when he went home and was the center of a whole lot of ridicule for being the odd one out. The combination of his elf and human DNA turned parts of his hair blue and made him stand out from the rest of his family. He hated holiday pictures which, for the Klausons, were mandatory.

He didn't say that. In fact, he was kind of blown away that Zeph liked it... liked him. Then he recalled what had been shouted through the door.

"Who is that Dan-thingy guy?"

"Danjal? He's my cousin."

Wow. Two angels in the same house? This is one hell of a weird day.

They made their way back, and Nick ignored Bob's smirking. So what if it wasn't their bathroom and they'd had mutually satisfying orgasms against a stranger's sink? *Sue us if it matters*. His gaze took in a messy office, a small furry animal that appeared from down the side of the sofa, Bob, Sam, and some guy with horns and red eyes. Where was Danjal?

Then it hit him as Zeph embraced the guy. This was Danjal? Danjal wasn't an angel but was in fact a freaking demon. A real one. Not a half demon, or a blood demon, but an honest-to-God, from-Hell demon. He took a step back but stopped when he bumped into Bob behind him. Sam was grinning at Danjal, Zeph was hugging him, and as for Bob? He was still chuckling. The fucker. The small furry animal—*is that a ferret?*—scampered between his legs and Bob's and was out the door in a flash. Sam and Bob took chase and abruptly there were only three of them left in the room.

"Nick, I want you to meet my cousin, Danjal Naamah."

Nick shook hands with him quickly, then dropped the grip just as quickly. He'd heard stories about full demons and all the freaky stuff they got up to.

"Hi, Nick," Danjal said with a smile. "How do you know this big idiot here?" He nodded his head to indicate Zeph. Nick closed his eyes briefly and waited for angel vengeance to smite the demon. When he heard nothing, he opened his eyes again to see Zeph and Danjal looking at him weirdly.

"Are you okay?" Zeph asked gently. He turned to the demon and said thoughtfully, "We just had sex so he may be a little overwhelmed."

Danjal chuckled and poked Zeph in the chest. "You can't go around saying things like that, *birdy*," he said firmly. "We don't talk about sex here like that." He turned to Nick. "It's nice to meet my cousin's mate," he said with a small bow.

Nick let out a squeak of protest. *Mate? What the hell?*

"He didn't know about that part," Zeph said quickly. He gripped Nick's hand tight, as if he was worried Nick would run. He was right—Nick wanted to run back to the bathroom pretty damn quick.

"Oh, sorry," Danjal grimaced. "My bad."

Zeph encouraged Nick to sit on the wide sofa and patted his hand. "Would you like a drink?" He poured golden liquid from a crystal decanter and placed the glass next to the ugliest looking gargoyle table decoration that Nick had ever seen. "We'll talk in a bit," he said gently. Then he ran a hand through Nick's hair, across that damn blue stripe, and placed a kiss on his head.

"So you wanted to see me?" Danjal asked. He'd sat on another chair and had his own glass of the liquid fire that

Nick had just had his first swallow of. He wondered if the old whiskey burned inside a demon the same way it burned inside him.

"Reports reached Raphael's desk about the brimstone incident. They sent me to check it out."

Danjal shrugged. "I wasn't going to sit around waiting to fill in forms to save children's lives," he said simply. He stared right at Zeph, and there was stubborn determination written on his face.

"I got you off with a fine," Zeph said immediately. "Passing your relationship with a wolf shifter may prove to be a little harder for me to fix."

"Wait a minute," Danjal said, irritated. "I expected shit about the brimstone, but now they're meddling in my love life?"

"Danjal—"

"No. You're saying it's okay with the angels that I use Hell's weapon, but they're not keen on me sleeping with Hart? That's bullshit."

Zeph shook his head sadly. "You know what they're like."

For a second, Nick thought things were going to come to blows. Danjal was spitting fire. Literally. There were now two round burn holes in the old patterned carpet. It was okay, though—Nick managed to stamp them out before they spread. Zeph stood, implacable and silent, obviously waiting for his cousin to get everything off his chest and work his way through anger to a place for rational discussion.

"What do they want?" Danjal finally asked with resignation.

"The usual."

"I am not going to visit Dad." Danjal sounded horrified.

Nick knew he'd have the same reaction if he were made to visit his own dad. Maybe Danjal was as much a disappointment to his dad as Nick was to his. Never good enough, not elf enough, not putting on weight even though Nick's mom made meals fit for a football team at each sitting. Then to turn out to be gay when he'd been in line for promotion to assistant Santa? That had been the nail in the coffin. Assistant Santas needed *Mrs.* Assistant Santas. His dad had never recovered from the fact that his only son would never get on the Klauson board.

Zeph held up a hand. "Once, Dan. He wants to see you and Hart together."

"So he can drive a wedge and tell Hart that he's polluting the natural angel/demon selection process? Hell no."

"He says he wants to meet Hart and give him his blessing."

Danjal muttered and ran a hand through his hair in frustration.

"Zeph, can't you—?"

"No. I just need an answer to take home."

"Okay. Okay! We'll do it. Freaking angels and their fluffy white soft shit."

Nick looked from Danjal, who was gorgeous and sexy and all kinds of bad, to Zeph who looked like purity, even dressed as he was in leather jacket and scruffy jeans. Then in a surprising move, Zeph pulled Danjal into a tight hug.

"I've missed you, Dan," he said fondly.

"Yeah, yeah." Danjal smirked. Then he tightened the hug. "I missed you too."

"When do I get to meet Hart?"

"He's dropping his daughter off at a werewolf winter camp where they'll teach her how to hunt in nature under safe conditions or some crap like that. When he comes back, we can all meet up." Danjal looked directly at Nick, who squirmed in his seat. Meet up with the demon again? Hell, he was having enough issues with meeting Zeph and *he* was an angel.

They parted from the hug and suddenly Zeph was all serious. "I need your help with a problem we have."

"I'm listening," Danjal said.

"We have a necromancer on the loose, and I could do with some of your location skills."

Danjal nodded his agreement immediately.

Nick let out a wide yawn. "Sorry," he apologized. "Been a long day."

Zeph smiled and offered a hand, which Nick held and used to stand. "Go get some sleep. I'll be up later."

Just like that, Nick was dismissed. But that was okay. Zeph said he'd be up later.

Even as sleep pulled Nick under, he desperately attempted to stay awake to talk to Zeph, but he wasn't able. His last thought was of the sexy angel and the single word that could well determine the rest of his life.

Mate.

Chapter Seven

ZEPH STARED AT THE FLOOR AND EXAMINED HIS SHOES AS Danjal talked at him. He really needed to get them shined.

"You can't just ignore me," Danjal cautioned. "You know you're going to have to let Nick go. They aren't going to like you bonding with whatever he is any more than my father likes me bonding with a wolf. Your brothers are going to lose it."

Zeph groaned. "I can't help it. He's the one."

"You mean *the one*—as in 'you're going to keep him and go against the angel council' type of *one*? Or the 'once you get him out of your system you can move on' type of one."

"As in he's worth having my wings taken." Zeph swallowed back the nerves as he made his confession.

"Oh, Zeph, I hope you know what you're doing." The pity in Dan's voice made him want to recant the words, but he couldn't. He knew Nick was it for him, his one chance for happiness.

"Me too."

"What are you two doing in here messing up Sam's

office?" a transparent figure demanded. It floated a foot above the ground and glared at them disapprovingly.

Zeph scowled back at the ghost. "What are you doing here?"

"I live here!"

Danjal waved a hand. "This is Teddy. He's the resident ghost."

"I can take care of the little ghost problem for Sam," Zeph offered, eyeing the apparition with disfavor. He didn't approve of spirits hanging around. They were supposed to pass on, not linger around and bug others.

"No! That's all right!" The ghost shot through the ceiling, disappearing in seconds.

"Huh, I never tried that to get rid of the guy," Danjal admitted. "He's kind of bothersome, but he did find me the maps for my location spell last time."

Zeph recalled what the two of them should be doing, and that didn't mean talking over the Nick situation. "We need to do that location spell to find that necromancer."

"And Nick?"

"Once the necromancer is dealt with, Nick and I can concentrate on more important things."

"Like seeing what's beneath those tight pants of his?"

"They are tight, aren't they?" Zeph's wings appeared and vibrated in excitement.

"Don't do that. It's disturbing," Danjal snapped. "If I'm going to do a location spell, I'm going to need those maps again. They're on the second floor. Did Sam give you permission to perform magic in his house? He's kind of fussy about that."

Zeph frowned. "It's to stop a zombie infestation. Surely he's all right with that?"

Danjal shrugged. "I'm going to wait until they return so

we can ask." Then he added, "Speak of the devil." Zeph winced at the language as, arriving on cue, Sam and Bob walked into the room. Sam had the ferret tucked in the crook of his arm where the little creature wiggled as if trying to escape.

"Aw, look—how cute!" Danjal said.

A strange expression crossed Sam's face. "Great. He's yours." He handed the ferret over to Danjal.

For a moment, Zeph thought his cousin would refuse, but after holding the furry beast a moment, Danjal smiled. "He's awesome, thanks."

Sam clapped his hands together. "Done. Good. I'm going to bed."

"Oh, Sam, one thing! Zeph came up with the idea of me doing another location spell for the necromancer," Danjal said.

"What about the personal connection you need to do it? Last time you were able to hone in on Hartman's daughter by using Hartman himself. What will you use this time?" Sam asked.

Danjal's mouth formed an O. "Umm, that's a good question."

"You can use my connection to the dead," Zeph offered. "It might help ground you enough to narrow down the search."

"Maybe." Danjal shrugged. Zeph could tell his cousin wasn't sold on the idea.

"It won't hurt to try, right?"

Danjal was slow to answer. "No, I guess it won't hurt. Can I use your office?" he asked Sam.

"Sure—shout if you need anything. Bob and I are going to bed. It's been an exhausting day." Waving, Sam left with a smiling vampire.

Zeph figured they weren't just sleeping. Thinking of Nick in the bedroom upstairs by himself had Zeph anxious to get this entire thing over with so he could go join his lover.

He let images of Nick lying in bed play around in his head for a moment. A slap to the back of his skull snapped him out of his daydreams.

"Ow, why did you do that?" He glared at Danjal.

"Because you were getting a creepy expression and pumping out pheromones. I don't need to know my cousin is having sex. It's weird."

"Oh please—like you and Hartman are celibate," Zeph scoffed.

"I didn't say we weren't having sex. I said you don't need to know about it."

Zeph laughed. Demons were weird. "Fair enough. Now what do you need for this location spell?"

"I should have everything in my bag." Danjal held up his satchel.

"Good. Let's go get started." He had his own mate warming his bed and he wanted to get to him.

———

SAM CLIMBED INTO BED, waiting for Bob to join him.

"Do you think they'll be okay?" As soon as he'd left the angel and demon together, he wondered if they should've stayed to help.

Bob shook his head. "You saw them. They don't need us. Besides, Danjal won't want the distraction of two extra people watching him work. If we stayed, we might have been more of a nuisance than anything."

As the vampire climbed on the bed with him, Sam

wondered how his life had turned around so much in just a few months.

Bob froze. "In a good way, right?"

"Didn't I tell you to stay out of my head?" Sam scolded without heat.

"Yes, you did, but I'll tell you what I always do. I would never know how much you cared if I went by your words instead of your thoughts. I learn all the best stuff by what you don't say."

Sam blushed. He knew he didn't express his feelings very often. He sighed. "You are going to make me say it, aren't you?"

Bob examined the blanket on their bed with a fixed intensity. "I have no idea what you mean."

"I might not be able to read minds, but you are an open book. Fine." Sam rolled his eyes. "I love you. Happy?"

Bob's eyes sparkled with laughter. "After that heartfelt declaration, how could I not be?" The vampire leaped onto the bed, causing the mattress to bounce. Bob grabbed Sam's arms and pinned them over his head. "I adore you, my grumpy human. The words aren't necessary as long as I can feel the emotion. I know you adore me, and that is more important than all the verbiage in the world."

Sam smiled. He didn't know if he would ever get used to this new paranormal world he'd plunged into. He'd worked so hard to be human only to find out he never was.

"You will always be my little human." Bob rubbed noses with Sam.

"I'd watch that little talk if you want to get laid."

Bob kissed Sam's face in short playful busses of the lips. "There's nothing little about you in all the right places." Bob cupped Sam's balls. "Yes, very nice."

Sam laughed. Then he sobered. "We need to talk about

Mal. You know I'm not happy about her staying at that school."

"She's fine with the wards that Zeph put in place on the basement, and anyway—no school-talk in bed. In fact, if it doesn't involve us having sex or your complete and total adoration of me, I will consider it off topic and not worth listening to."

"Oh, is that how it's going to be?" Sam asked.

"Yep."

"And who elected you big man in charge?"

Sam could see the second Bob knew he'd made a tactical mistake, but Sam let him swing in the breeze a little longer.

"Now, baby, I didn't mean it that way."

Sam rolled them over and lightly pinned Bob to the mattress. It wasn't as if he could move the vampire if he resisted, but he liked being on top of Bob if only for a moment. "I like you on bottom."

"You like me any way you can get me," Bob retorted.

Sam pretended to consider that for a moment. "You know what? I really do."

He had intended the kiss to be fast and hard, but the events of the day rode Sam. If he'd lost Mal in the zombie attack, he never would've forgiven himself. "I can't lose you, Bob."

"You won't, babe. I'm harder to kill than you think."

Sam didn't even try to hide the emotion in his voice. "We've been through so much, and if anything happened to you, I would never get over the loss."

"Good," Bob replied smugly. "I like knowing you'd be mine even if I died."

"You wouldn't want me to go on and have a nice life?" Sam teased.

"Nope. Wallow in misery. That way no one else gets to

enjoy you." Bob flipped them back over. "Because you are mine in this life and the next. I've even got an angel and a demon in the house to confirm it. Once you die, I'm going to have your soul held until I can join you. You aren't even going to enter the afterlife without me by your side."

Bob sounded so certain—so completely convinced of their life together, Sam couldn't do anything but agree. "If you say so, Bob."

"I want you to practice that phrase. I like how it sounds on your lips. You can repeat it for anything," the vampire urged.

"Ah, I see. Very commanding of you."

"I'm a take-charge kind of guy." Bob agreed.

"Well, Mr. Take Charge, maybe you can make it your mission to get the lube because I don't care how sexy you are, there's no way I'm taking you dry."

"Good point." Bob reached across the bed and opened the side drawer. He snatched up the container and waved it victoriously.

"You got the lube out of the nightstand, you didn't run a marathon," Sam said dryly.

"Don't ruin my moment of success," Bob admonished.

The vampire scooped out a dollop of lube on one finger. He slid to Sam's right side to relieve Sam of the weight of his body. "Lift."

Sam obediently lifted his legs, exposing his hole for Bob. "I could roll over."

"No. I like you like this. It's like you're a sexy offering and I'm the god of love."

Sam grabbed his knees so he wouldn't topple over while he laughed.

Bob scowled at him. "It wasn't that funny!"

"I don't think I appreciated how hysterical you are until this moment."

The vampire slid his lubed finger into Sam's ass, pushing it in and out, loosening Sam up. He added more slick and widened Sam further.

"You ready for me, baby?"

"I'm ready, but don't call me baby."

Sam didn't know why he bothered. Bob used a million pet names for Sam and never did he stop using one just because it annoyed Sam. In fact, the more Sam hated it, the more Bob used it.

Bob coated his cock with lubricant. He steadied Sam with his hands on Sam's hips. "It's been a few hours since we had sex so I'm going to go slow."

"Not too slow." Sam flushed as memories of their hot encounter against the bathroom door flickered through his mind like a porn show.

"Oh yeah, think of that while I fuck you. That's so hot." Bob's voice deepened as he pushed inside of Sam.

Sam obediently tried to keep the memory going while Bob entered him.

Sam had showered, he'd been drying off and preparing to dress. He'd turned toward the door after brushing his teeth to find Bob leaning against it.

"Oh yeah, keep it going, babe. I like how you see me," Bob groaned as he slowly moved in and out of Sam's hole, keeping a gentle grip on Sam's legs to help keep him in position.

Sam relaxed his body as his memories flooded his mind.

Bob had grabbed Sam and swung them around. Where he'd found the lube Sam didn't know, but in seconds, Sam was prepped and ready and Bob was slamming him against the door.

Memories of Bob fucking him merged with the actual act. Sam couldn't stop his orgasm. His back bowed as he came, dragging Bob along with him.

"Oh fuck, that was good." Bob rested his forehead against Sam's. "I don't think I'll ever need porn again."

Sam laughed. Bob moved inside him, sending tiny aftershocks through his body.

Groaning, Bob slid out and tumbled over to lie beside him. "I love you too, sweetness."

"Thanks." Sam contemplated smothering the vampire with his pillow.

A loud banging on the door snapped Sam out of his happy post-coital cloud.

"Do you think we'll ever get to wallow in orgasmic bliss, or does everyone have to have an emergency after we have sex?" Bob asked.

Sam groaned. Crawling out of bed, he snatched up his robe before opening the door. He didn't bother checking on Bob. The vampire would either dress quickly or do some sneaky mind trick so the visitor thought he'd dressed.

"What's wrong?" Sam asked. The expression on Zeph's face sent a sinking sensation through Sam's stomach. His happy bliss sank faster than a stone in still water.

"It's Danjal. When he connected with the necromancer there were unexpected side effects," Zeph said. His wings fluttered behind him as if the nerves were conveyed through the motion.

"Give us a minute. We'll be right there."

Zeph nodded, then turned and ran.

Bob put a hand on Sam's shoulder. "I don't have a good feeling about this."

"Me either," Sam agreed. "Let's get clean, then we can decide how to deal with the latest crisis."

Bob froze in the act of putting on his shirt. "We do seem to be in a state of perpetual crisis, don't we?"

Sam nodded. "When I wanted to be a detective, I thought I'd be investigating other people's problems. I never suspected that they'd all become my own."

"Yeah. I didn't expect *you* either."

Their kiss, soft and gentle, was at complete odds to the urgency of the situation.

"We'd best go see what happened. Luckily, no one has burned down my house yet."

Before the words finished leaving Sam's lips, the fire alarm went off.

Bob's pitying look didn't help Sam's panic at all.

Chapter Eight

Zeph slid to a halt outside Nick's door. What if he couldn't contain the fire and the whole damned house burned down? Nick needed to know there was a problem. He opened the door and shouted Nick's name, and Nick sat upright in bed with shock carved on his face.

"We have a fire. You need to get out." Zeph had to shout over the top of the smoke alarm, but Nick heard him and was up and out of bed in an instant. Zeph grabbed his arm and dragged him down the stairs, his wings slightly unfurled in case there was fire anywhere that could hurt him. He pushed him toward the front door just as Sam and Bob arrived on the scene.

"What the hell?" Sam shouted loudly.

"Help me. Help me." The voice was faint, but Zeph could hear it and he plunged into the flames in the office. Danjal was still lying where Zeph had left him, unconscious and with flames licking from his body and up the wall.

"Over here!" the voice commanded. Zeph zeroed in on a gargoyle perched on the edge of the desk, looking ready to throw himself off. In a swift move, he scooped up the stone

being and rushed to pass it outside. Sam had an extinguisher and Bob had disappeared, which left Nick. He thrust the creature at Nick, who took it and stumbled backward at the sudden weight.

"What happened?" Nick shouted. Sam pushed past and snapped the chain on the extinguisher before aiming it at the walls. There was no smoke. There wouldn't be—this was Hell's fire crawling and creeping along wall and carpet, curling mischievous threads of fire that spun and burned a trail from Danjal's unconscious form.

"Is there anyone else in here?" Zeph asked Sam urgently. Bob appeared at his side with another extinguisher. "Any others still in there I need to get out?"

"No. Smudge isn't here. He…" Sam looked confused, then seemed to shake it free. "No, there's no one."

Zeph pushed Sam back and ignored Bob's snarl of warning. He glanced at Nick who was clearly in shock. "All three of you outside. Now." Something flew between his legs in a streak of brown and he twisted to watch as the ferret that Danjal had held stopped dead in front of his cousin and buried his face in his paws. A strange keening sound, a mix of whine and growl, emanated from the ferret and it crawled carefully between flames to curl into Danjal's side. Zeph knew there and then that this was a matched familiar and would die with Danjal before leaving. *Two lives he had to save.*

He shoved at Sam again until they were clear of the doorway, then pushed the door close as far as he could. The heat in the room was intense, and Zeph wished he didn't have to do this, but there was only one way to cool Danjal down and save his cousin's life and that of his little familiar. The Council was not going to be happy, but what the hell. He was already going to be in deep shit for whatever he had with Nick. Why not add aiding and abetting a demon to the list?

He stumbled over a chair that had fallen over and got caught up in the maps on the floor—or at least what remained of them. Spreading his wings wide, he crouched next to Danjal and pulled and pushed at him until he was curled on his side in a fetal position. His eyes were wide and vacant and the blood red in them seemed to be growing. They didn't have long before the hellfire and brimstone turned on the one who wielded the power and burnt Danjal to nothing but dust. Flexing his wings, he covered his cousin entirely, then he bent his head and began a series of incantations that he recalled from an earlier time when demons and angels were mortal enemies.

If anything, the heat increased and Zeph felt his wings begin to spark at the edges. Feathers he could grow back, but the heart of him being lost in demonic fire was something he would never recover. He focused on the magic that had caused this. They'd been so close. Danjal had narrowed a location to a suburb of the city and was so close when he cursed.

"He's shielding from me," he'd said. There hadn't been fear in Danjal's voice, just curiosity. There wasn't much that could hide from a demon or an angel.

"How is he doing that?"

Danjal had shaken his head. "He can only be using stolen celestial magic."

Fear had frozen Zeph in place at Danjal's words. A necromancer with magic that strong was someone to fear.

When Danjal had abruptly arched away from the maps with a scream and fell back writhing to the floor, Zeph had tried to cool the magic, but it was too late. All too quickly, hellfire and brimstone tumbled through the link and Danjal was consumed. Zeph had disconnected any link he could, but Danjal had already been on fire.

Each piece of his clothing was burning away, but his skin and form remained untouched. He had natural barriers to fire, but this was too much.

"*You can't get him back,*" the words echoed in the room and were accompanied by a cackle of laughter. "*I sent his fire back to him threefold.*" The cackle turned, and instead of laughter, there was now superior smugness. "*Your shield to the fire is too much for you to summon his mate in time.*"

Zeph pushed a barrier in place to stop the words and the fire died a little. The necromancer was somehow still connected to Danjal. He closed his eyes. What did the necromancer mean about Hartman? Mate magic? The purity of connection? Zeph tried to find Hartman, but he was overwhelmed by the fire—there was no way he could get Hartman in time.

Nick. What if the connection between him and Zeph, although in its infancy, was enough to block the link between the necromancer and Danjal?

"I'm here." Nick's voice was at his side. The room burned around him, but he showed no sign of fear. Zeph lifted a wing and Nick climbed under until he was huddled with Danjal and the little ferret. Could this be enough? Zeph touched Nick— fear at what could happen enough to almost make him stop.

"Nick, I can't…"

"I can feel Danjal's despair, his fear. Let me help," Nick demanded. Then he closed his eyes and his face was free from fear or worry.

Mate.

Drawing every ounce of energy from the connection to Nick, he forced his will on the link and abruptly it snapped and the cackle of laughter in his head was silenced. The heat in the room died a little, but instead of hellfire, it was small flames of natural energy.

"You can come in," Zeph called to Sam and Bob. They ran in with the extinguishers and finished every single flame they could find. Sodden and steaming, the carpet was finished and the only water-free zone was beneath Zeph's wings.

Nick opened his eyes and looked up at Zeph. "Did we do it?"

Zeph nodded and slowly retracted his singed wings. "We did." He stepped back and held out a hand to help Nick to his feet. The ferret burrowed next to the now peacefully sleeping Danjal. Zeph leaned down and touched his cousin, and with a muttered incantation, Danjal and the ferret disappeared.

"Where did you send him?" Nick asked carefully.

Zeph closed his eyes briefly in concentration. "To his mate. He needs his wolf now."

"Will he be okay?" Bob asked. "He saved Mal's life."

Sam nodded and leaned against Bob. "He's a good guy."

Zeph pulled Nick close and said over his head. "Danjal will be okay."

"What now?" Nick asked against Zeph's chest. "There goes our chance of tracking the thing who is doing all of this."

"We managed to get something. We narrowed it down to Crestville."

Sam looked shocked. "Near the school? The damn thing is right near Mal's school?" He looked at Bob. "We're going now."

Bob didn't argue. "Two minutes to get dressed," he said firmly. "Then, angel, you need to zap us to where we need to be."

Nick wriggled out of Zeph's hold. "I'm coming too."

Zeph nodded. "Two minutes. When the link to Danjal

snapped, it would have hurt him badly. We need to use that to our advantage."

Bob and Sam ran from the room, and Nick followed them. Suddenly, it was just him standing in the darkened room.

"Not just you," a voice he recognized called from the floor. He looked down at the gargoyle waddling into the room. Even on its stony face, he could see sadness. "He burned my home," the stone creature said. "Can you put me back?"

Zeph picked him up and pushed aside smoldering remnants of papers and placed him on the corner. "What is your name?" Zeph asked curiously. He normally knew everything about someone by touch, yet he couldn't sense anything in this small being.

"No one has ever asked me that," the gargoyle said. "But my name means nothing to anyone."

"You won't tell me."

"I can't." With that, the gargoyle resumed its stone state and there was no more conversation to be had. Zeph looked around the ruined room to see if anything needed to be done before he left, but there was no sign of heat. With a final touch to the gargoyle's head, he left the room and shut the door. The scent of brimstone filled the house, but with a click of his finger, the smell dissipated and the only thing left behind was the scent of lemons.

This had to stop. Someone was going to pay for what they'd done to Danjal.

NICK HELD out a hand and placed it in Zeph's, then linked with Bob. In a circle with Sam completing the connection, he waited for whatever happened next. He'd never traveled by angel before, and he would be lying if he said he wasn't worried. There was no indication they had even moved, but when Nick blinked, he was in a different place. A shadowy wood with trees gnarled in age. The despair in this place was overwhelming, and for a second, he had to bend at the waist to get his head to stop spinning. Zeph touched him on the back and smoothed small circles into his skin. The touch settled him. After a moment, he straightened.

"How far are we away from the school?" Sam asked.

"Maybe ten minutes' walk," Zeph said. He spun in a slow circle and shuddered. Nick understood what his angel was sensing. Evil so dark it permeated through the trees and the plants. Everything here was dying.

"I want to get Mal out of the school." Bob stated unequivocally.

Sam instantly nodded. "I agree."

"In fact, we should get all the kids to a safe place," Bob added. "I don't know how many there were, but we have a large house, we can hide them there."

Nick instinctively knew this was the wrong move. The despair and hate he felt in this wooded area was more than he'd ever felt. Zeph's protection remained in place around the school, and he just knew they were safer there.

"No," he said quickly.

"She's our daughter," Sam said sharply.

"And she's safer at the school. I think we should let Zeph do his thing."

Bob crossed his arms over his chest. "So what is it you think we should do?" The question was for Zeph, and Nick wasn't affronted that Bob had turned to Zeph for a decision. After all, it was what he would do. He certainly wouldn't rely on the word of a half-elf.

"Ouch," he said as Zeph smacked him upside the head. "What was that for?"

"Your instincts are good," Zeph snapped. "Stop second-guessing yourself." Then he shook his wings, unfurling them gracefully. Nick could see the tinge of black on the very edges and felt sad for what had happened. He forced it down. If Zeph could read his thoughts, then he wanted to convey absolute trust and happiness and nothing else.

"We'll need to do it this way. Bob, I need your stealth skills and ability to see in the dark. Sam, I need you to…" He trailed off and tilted his head at Sam. "I need you to stay with Bob at all times."

Nick frowned. What happened there? It was almost as if Zeph was going to hand out an assignment, then changed his mind.

"He's too important to us all for us to show our hand now." Zeph's words filtered into Nick's head.

"Nick, I need you to track the worst of all of this. Together we can find the necromancer and together we will defeat him."

Zeph strode off down the path.

Nick couldn't help but think how magnificent his angel looked.

Chapter Nine

SAM DIDN'T LIKE THE FOREST. HE HAD THE IMPRESSION IF HE listened a little harder the trees would start a conversation with him.

"Trees can't talk, Sam," Bob said beside him.

"Says you. I've had some weird crap happen lately. I wouldn't be the least surprised if they decided to speak. It would probably be one of the *least* strange things that've happened to me."

After all, he was following an angel, a half-elf, and a vampire into a haunted forest. He wondered if he should start writing horror novels. He could base them on his own happy experiences.

"Someday soon, I'm going to get a paying gig," Sam muttered. "One that doesn't involve my possible death."

"You got paid by Hartman and that troll," Bob reminded him. The amused tone in his mate's voice didn't reassure Sam. Bob didn't appear to take his concerns seriously. "Relax, mate, I have plenty of money."

Sam wasn't even going to respond to that. He wasn't.

"I'm not living off you."

Okay, he couldn't help it.

Bob chuckled beside him.

A cold wind rushed through the forest, biting through Sam's jacket like siren teeth. He shivered from the chill. None of the leaves moved.

"Did you feel that?"

Bob frowned. "What?"

"That breeze."

"Sam, there isn't a breeze."

Sam's hair ruffled. He raised an eyebrow at Bob. "Really?"

Bob stared at him. "Huh. That isn't natural."

"How odd. I never have strange things happen to me."

"Sarcasm doesn't answer the problem, love."

"No, but it makes me feel better."

"What are you two doing?" Zeph traced his path back to them.

"Sam here seems to be having an encounter of the spiritual sort."

Another puff of air whipped around Sam.

"Okay, I felt that one," Bob said.

"Me too," Nick piped up beside them.

"I think it's coming from over there." Sam pointed to the south. Was it his imagination, or was the forest darker over there?

"No, it's darker," Bob agreed.

"Hmm." Sam took a deep breath. Now wasn't the time to become afraid of the dark. Not with everything he'd already encountered. Somehow that one patch of dark forest gave him the willies more than a basement of zombies. Sadly, he had the experience to compare the two.

"Well, let's check it out." Bob slipped his hand into Sam's, giving it a reassuring squeeze as he led Sam forward.

It took concentrated effort not to dig in his heels and refuse to go. He didn't like anything about this situation. Only the fact he had so many powerful paranormals by his side had him agreeing to go along. Sam had decided two almost-death encounters ago that he really wasn't that brave.

"You're braver than you know," Bob soothed. He ran his hand down Sam's back as if he could infuse Sam with more bravery with his touch.

"There isn't time for a panic attack," Zeph said, scowling at them.

"Nonsense, there is always time for a panic attack." Sam grinned at Zeph. Baiting the winged man cheered Sam up immensely.

"You are a funny almost human," a whispery voice said.

Everyone froze where they stood.

Sam squinted into the dark woods. He wished he had night vision like the vampire beside him. Light flooded the forest. Sam blinked at the sudden brilliance.

"What happened?" Nick asked.

"Sam?" Bob turned to look at him. "What did we say about wishing?"

"Oops?" Sam blushed as all attention turned toward him. "What? It doesn't always work."

He wasn't going to justify his freaky powers. He didn't understand them so how could he explain them to anyone else.

Nick surveyed the brightly lit woods. "That's awesome."

Sam smiled. At least one person wasn't looking at him like he was weird.

The soft whispering began again. Sam couldn't make out the words, but he could feel the intent. She wanted him to follow. Stepping away from Bob, Sam trailed after the whispery voice. What she said he didn't know, but he could feel her intentions were good.

The forest dimmed from a blinding brilliance to a twilight glow. Bright enough to see but not so he'd need sunglasses. A mist formed in front of him. The white fog shimmered and twisted until it grew into the shape of a winged woman. She wore jeans and a red tank top and her mouth drooped at the corners in a sorrow so palpable Sam had to blink away the tears.

"I am here," she whispered.

Sam looked at the ground below where she floated. A plain gray rock stood in place of a headstone with nothing written on it. The newly turned earth revealed she couldn't have been dead for long.

"Ariel, is that you?" Zeph asked. His tone hushed.

"Zeph! I'm sorry." She looked broken, her anguish palpable. "I should've listened to you."

"I told you he wasn't good for you!" Zeph said.

The apparition's wings dipped down farther. "I know. I thought he loved me. Instead he stole my magic and killed my body."

"Why would he do that?" Sam asked. He'd never heard of anyone stealing angel magic before. The angel's expression of deep sorrow twisted Sam's heart. He couldn't help wanting to ease Ariel's sadness. He'd become a detective to help people with their problems—he just hadn't thought he'd end up helping the dead.

"He keeps me here because he didn't know I was his soul mate. He thinks if he can bind me to one location, he won't feel the pain of losing his other half."

Sam assessed the condition of the woods. "That's why he turned, isn't it? He's trying to bring you back."

The necromancer's obsession with reviving the dead

made sense once Sam realized his motivation. When he'd destroyed Ariel, it had probably turned a man who leaned toward the evil side of the spectrum completely insane.

"Yes," the floating angel said. "He's trying to bring me back."

"Where is he? Is he still here?"

Ariel shook her head. "He left before you came here. The connection to me was snapping and he had to go."

Sam wasn't sure whether to be relieved that the necromancer had left or scared about where the hell he'd gone. "What do we do now?"

"You can't resurrect an angel," Zeph said.

The angel nodded her agreement. "He didn't believe me when I told him that. He tried everything to become all-powerful—using the ancient dead in the school, and he even attempted a dragon's magic."

"We know," Bob said dryly.

"He's the only thing holding me here, using my powers against me. If he lets me go, he'll lose my magic with me. He now wants me and my magic, and he's willing to destroy everyone to get it."

"What usually happen when an angel dies?" Sam asked.

"We return to our pool of celestial magic to be reborn," Zeph explained.

"So you don't really die, you just get recycled," Sam said. An image of a giant sparkling pool of liquid magic slid into his mind. As he watched, an angel stepped out of the pool shining with power as if lit from inside. He shook his head to dispel the strange image.

"From what I understand, that is pretty much close to reality," Bob said.

"Stop reading my mind." Sam didn't know why he even

bothered anymore. His lover considered Sam's brain his own personal playground.

"But how would I figure out what you were thinking? It's not like you share."

Sam sighed. "Can we focus on the problem? Not that you're a problem."

The angel nodded her understanding. Even dead, her tragic beauty tugged at Sam's heart. He bet when she'd lived she'd been gorgeous.

Bob pinched him.

"Ouch."

"Don't think of other people like that."

Sam rolled his eyes. "We should get out of here. Now that we know his motivation, maybe we can figure out how to fight him."

"How do we take her with us?" Nick asked. "Isn't she tied to her grave?"

Ariel floated over to Sam and took his hand.

Sam shivered from the chill of her touch. "I guess she's coming with me."

The group moved away from the grave with the ghost floating by his side like she was a balloon on a string and he was pulling her along. When it appeared they were far enough away for Zeph to do what he did best, Sam knew he had to do one more thing. He glanced at Bob who nodded in agreement.

"We're checking in on Mal," Sam said firmly.

"See if she's okay," Bob added.

Zeph scowled at them. "You can't go," he pointed at Sam. "You can't take a ghost through the wards I put near the school."

"I'll go then." Bob crossed his arms over his chest and

stared at Zeph. His expression was the stubborn one that Sam often encountered.

"This isn't necessary," Zeph said with a touch of impatience. "I can assure you that your daughter is safe, as are the other children."

"But they're small," Ariel whispered into Sam's ear. "Zephariel could get there and back in a blink of an eye."

Sam heard what she said. "Go and check on the children," he said. "Please," he added gently.

"That will leave you unprotected here." Zeph immediately turned to Nick, and there was such a look of intense fear in the angel's eyes that Sam knew Zeph and Nick were bonded. There was a connection between them that reminded Sam of himself and Bob.

"I'll be okay," Nick protested. Zeph grimaced, then in the blink of an eye, he grabbed at Nick's arm and the two of them disappeared.

"He took Nick," Bob commented to no one in particular.

"He didn't want to leave him here," Sam observed. "Probably because of the axe-wielding murderer on the loose in the trees." As soon as he said the words, spoken in jest, he realized what he'd said. He scooted closer to Bob and shivered as Ariel moved with him. They stood like this for maybe five minutes, then with a flash of electric sparks, Nick and Zeph arrived back in the clearing.

"Are they okay?" Bob asked quickly.

"Every child is asleep in bed with my blessing upon them," Zeph said grandly.

"Thank goodness," Sam muttered. Bob gripped his hand and they exchanged grateful glances.

"Each child is dreaming of happy things," Zeph added. As he said it, he looked at Nick, and Sam had to stifle a snort of laughter. Big, bad angel was trying his utmost to impress the elf. Then Sam noticed something else—Zeph's words might well be sweeping but he could only use one arm to emphasize them.

"What is that?" Sam asked curiously. It looked as if Zeph had bought back something from the school? "Is that a rock or something?"

Zeph shook his head. "He wanted to come with us."

"He?" Sam asked, but even as he asked, he knew damn well what Zeph had under his arm. "You're not taking that back to my house. I already have one grumpy gargoyle to deal with." At that moment, the stone morphed and cracked and the biggest stone eyes looked up at Sam. Hell, since when did gargoyles use the stone equivalent to puppy-eyes?

"Please, Sam-non-human, I have things to tell you."

"What?"

If anything, the little gargoyle looked even more pathetic and big-eyed. Sam melted a little on the inside. Maybe this was just a baby gargoyle. Were there even baby gargoyles? How did gargoyles make babies?

"Don't think about that," Bob groaned and pressed fingertips to his temples. "I won't be able to get that out of my head now."

Sam smirked. "Served you right for being in my head," he said with a laugh. Shaking his head, he reached out and touched the stone creature and a gasp of pleasure drifted up to him on the air. Then he sighed loudly. "Zeph, get us all home."

NICK DIDN'T KNOW what to make of this group of people he'd fallen in with. The vampire made the most sense to him because he'd dealt with them in the past. Zeph had him tied up in knots and the only emotion he could feel toward Sam was total fear. The almost human had powers far above any supernatural Nick had ever met. Frankly, Sam scared the sugar cookies out of Nick.

They returned to Sam's office building. A rush of joy poured through Nick as Sam stepped across the threshold. Nick paused in his own entering. The hall lights brightened and the ambience turned joyful the more Sam walked into the hall, as if the property embraced its owner's return.

"Is it always like that?" Nick whispered to Bob.

The vampire nodded. "He never seems to notice."

"Huh." Sam was probably the most oblivious man Nick had ever met. He didn't appear to see when things changed around him, or maybe so many strange things happened, he just didn't notice anymore. Nick wasn't the type to judge others, but Sam interested him. Apparently, he interested the angel ghost too because she hadn't left his side since they decided to take her with them. As to the newest addition to the party, the tiny stone gargoyle, he wasn't sure where to file that one. It had fallen asleep in Zeph's arms, and he'd placed it carefully on Sam's desk with a soft huff of approval. Seeing his angel handling something so gently reminded him of their first kiss. A quick glance showed the original gargoyle hadn't reanimated.

They gathered around Sam's office. Before they could start their impromptu meeting, a large wolf stomped into the room. The beast plopped down beside Sam and growled.

"I'm sorry, Hartman. I didn't know the necromancer would hurt Dan," Sam apologized immediately.

"This is Hartman?" Zeph approached the wolf cautiously. "Hi! I'm Dan's cousin, Zeph. It's nice to meet you."

The wolf stared at Zeph with indifference. Nick thought he heard the beast snort.

"I'm sure he's happy to meet you too," Sam interjected. "He's just upset about Dan."

"Is Dan okay?"

Right there in the middle of Sam's office, the wolf shifted into human. At least that's what Nick thought happened. Halfway through the change, Zeph clapped a hand over Nick's eyes.

"What are you doing?"

"You don't need to see my cousin's mate naked."

"What about you?"

"I'm an angel."

"So?"

"I'm used to seeing people in their natural born state."

"There are clothes in the guest room. Go put them on," Bob ordered.

Apparently the vampire didn't like Sam seeing the wolf shifter naked either if his disapproving tone was anything to go by.

"I have seen him naked before," Sam said. Nick could hear the amusement in Sam's voice.

Zeph removed his hand from Nick's eyes. There was no sign of the shifter. He must've gone to dress.

"We'll wait until Hart returns. Maybe he has something to add," Sam said.

"Or maybe he just wants to yell at us all for endangering his mate," Bob growled.

Sam shrugged. "Maybe." He didn't appear overly concerned about the matter, and Nick noticed that Zeph was just as calm. Evidently both of them felt they could handle one seriously pissed off wolf.

Hart returned before speculation could become too wild. "Why did you send home a ferret?" he demanded.

"Your mate was wounded and you're worried about a ferret?" Nick asked.

The shifter's nose twitched. "Why do you smell like candy canes?"

Nick rolled his eyes. Shifters and their damn noses. "Because I'm related to Santa. Happy?"

Hart turned his attention to Sam. "He's kidding, right?"

Sam shook his head. "I don't think so."

"An angel, a vampire, an elf, and whatever the fuck you are. It's like the beginning of a bad joke," Hart commented, looking from one person to another. "And an angel ghost. Sorry, ma'am, I didn't see you at first."

Nick hid his smile by turning away slightly. Hart was right about one thing, they were a motley collection of people. However, he doubted they would be able to beat a necromancer without a variety of skills.

Sam continued, "This is Nick. Zeph, your cousin-in-law, and our ghost here is Ariel who was killed by the necromancer for her power. She suspects the necromancer didn't realize she was his soul mate when he killed her and now he keeps bringing things back to life to eventually return her to the living."

"That's fucked up." Hart glared at them. "What can I do to help? He messed with Dan; he needs to die."

Nick had to admire the shifter's simplistic view of the world. Hartman didn't appear concerned about right or wrong, only that his mate had been injured.

He wondered how Zeph would react if something happened to Nick. Would his mate be out for blood, or would his sense of right and wrong be stronger than his loyalty to his lover? Nick hoped he'd never have to find out.

Chapter Ten

His phone rang just as Nick climbed into bed. He'd left Zeph and Ariel chatting in the office, with Sam snoring on the sofa and Bob keeping guard. Seemed Ariel couldn't leave Sam's side, and as she and Zeph had a lot to cover, Sam was stuck where he was. Of course Bob was inches from his side. Disappointment flooded him. Zeph had just said Nick should go get some sleep, even when he'd offered to stay.

One moment, Nick had felt as if it was possible Zeph *was* his fated mate as he kept dramatically declaring. In that single shining moment, Nick had felt wanted and needed, and that he was better than his family told him he was. Of course it hadn't lasted long. Too many years of being told he wasn't a real Klauson had been enough to give him a severe case of low self-esteem.

He answered the call and immediately wished he hadn't.

"Little cousin!" Edmund's voice was deep and loud, and Nick wouldn't have been surprised if he hadn't added a *ho ho ho* on the end. Edmund was 100 percent Klauson, full white beard and rounded tummy all ready for when it was his turn to take a place in the family business. At the moment,

Edmund was a low-level manager, but he was destined for big things. "You done there yet?"

"Not exactly," Nick answered quickly. "Things are more complicated than we first thought."

"You're needed back here. There's black spot reports coming in all over the city and the team needs your help."

Nick didn't say a word. He could feel the despair seeping through the night sky and not even the mention of actually being needed by anyone back home got him to smile.

"I'll be home when I'm finished here," Nick said firmly. Edmund was one of those people who felt like he was in charge simply by virtue of the fact he was a year older, forever ordering Nick around and commenting on his impure bloodline. Edmund never came out and said the words directly, but he would slyly insert the meaning into something else. Nick crossed to the window and rested his forehead on the cool glass.

Edmund sighed noisily. "I don't know what Dad will say. He's already pissed that you aren't getting the job done."

"Santa is, or you are?" Nick asked quickly.

"I'm sorry," Edmund responded. He sighed again. "I know it's wrong for us to expect you to be able to handle everything alone. I get that your skills are a little lacking…"

Nick bit his lip to stop himself from saying something, but he couldn't stop the tension in his head. One day, he would snap and not a single one of his cousins would know what the hell hit them.

He started in surprise when Zeph appeared and grabbed the phone from him.

"Who is this?" he demanded. A frown furrowed his forehead, but Nick couldn't hear whatever Edmund was saying, if indeed he was saying anything.

"Give me the phone," Nick pleaded. The last thing he

needed was Zeph causing waves.

Zeph raised a hand, then placed it palm down on Nick's chest. Sudden peace washed over Nick, and he stumbled backward to sit on the bed. He felt like his legs couldn't support him. Edmund had clearly answered Zeph's demand for his name with a request of his own. Zeph's wings extended and cast a shadow over Nick as they blocked the small ceiling light. Nick had never seen anything so magnificent in his life.

With a voice that shook the room and a flash of silver in his eyes, Zeph told Edmund who he was in no uncertain terms. "I am Zephariel, Angel of Vengeance," he announced. "You show your cousin no respect," he added. "Do you know what he is capable of?" Nick could vaguely hear shouting at the other end. Was it just him, or did Edmund's voice have a tinge of fear in it? "Listen to me, elf. Nick's human side makes him stronger than any of your clan. You will respect him." Zeph's voice had a growly edge to it, and Nick couldn't help the fact that suddenly he was incredibly turned on by what he was hearing. Zeph with wings extended and utter faith in Nick was a sight to behold—sexy, strong, and in control.

Zeph glanced at Nick, then smiled and handed the cell phone to Nick. "He wants to talk to you."

Nick took the innocent looking piece of technology. "Hello?"

"Who the hell... What... Nick..." Edmund was manifestly lost for words.

"He's my fated mate," Nick said firmly. Then he cut off the call without a good-bye. He didn't want to lose the passion inside him in meaningless conversation with a cousin who needed to get a life. Very deliberately, he crossed to Zeph who, to be honest, looked a little sheepish.

"They hate that I'm half human, you know. Made me think like I didn't belong," Nick said with a shrug. "And then I met you. You said I was strong. You came to help me."

Zeph grasped one of Nick's hands briefly, and his wings gradually closed in tight to his back and disappeared. "I will always be there for you."

Nick shook free of Zeph's grasp and instead closed his hands around the back of Zeph's neck. They kissed and sudden contentment replaced lust. "Make love to me," he pleaded.

Zeph scooped Nick up into his arms and deposited him gently on the wide bed. With a flick of his fingers, he was gloriously naked, his cock hard and lust written on his expression. He crawled onto the bed and helped Nick scoot back until Nick had his head on the soft pillows.

"The door," Nick said in sudden worry. Another click and the door locked. Nick huffed a laugh. "Can you magic lube?"

"Let me worry about that," Zeph said, smiling. Then he began to kiss a path from ear to throat, and Nick realized he was too far gone in wanting Zeph to even care how they got lube. This was it—this was him being with a partner who would be right for him. They kissed lazily. Zeph didn't use his powers to strip Nick, instead he revealed Nick's body layer by layer and kissed every inch of the exposed skin. A spark flickered above them with every kiss and the light dimmed until a cocoon of half dark surrounded them.

"I have waited millennia for you," Zeph whispered. He pressed his body close and abruptly there was skin on skin contact. Nick arched up into the weight. Fear spiraled inside him. Did a mere mortal survive making love with an angel and his celestial magic? *Would it ever be more than this once?*

Zeph reared back in sudden shock.

"What?" Nick asked desperately. He didn't want this to stop. Why was Zeph stopping?

"Angels have been mated with humans since time began," Zeph said gently. "When the…" He paused as if searching for the precise word. "When the *connection* is as strong as ours, when you know it is absolutely perfect and real, then love is a protective shield that shelters us both." He extended his wings above them, and Nick couldn't help himself. He stroked the closest part of them he could reach, and Zeph shuddered under the touch.

"Does it hurt?" Nick asked gently.

"If you don't stop, this could be over before it starts."

"Oh." He dropped his touch immediately, and Zeph kissed him in thanks. He wriggled until his own cock rested against Zeph's and gently he rocked upward. Zeph muttered something in a language Nick had never heard, then threw his head back and closed his eyes as they moved together. Nick rolled them and sat to straddle Zeph. "I wasn't joking about the lube," he said seriously. "If I don't get you inside me soon, I may have to rub myself off on you."

Zeph coated his hands in a liquid that sparkled and appeared from nowhere, and Nick got with the plan immediately. He lifted himself a little, and Zeph pressed his fingers against Nick. The touch was electric, and Nick keened as Zeph prepared him. While Zeph held still, Nick lowered down onto Zeph's cock and, in a smooth motion, he was filled. There was no pain, nothing except sensation and the feeling of absolute connection. For a second, he stopped and stared down at Zeph's face.

"I've never…" he began. He didn't have the words to explain how he felt at this moment—in awe of what he was being given, and loved by an angel who said he was better than he thought.

"Me neither," Zeph said softly. Then he moved a little and sensations chased through Nick's body like warm fire in his veins. "Okay?" Zeph asked, concern in his voice.

"More," Nick demanded. Zeph smiled up at him and curled his body up to clasp Nick close. He was strong and steady, and Nick relaxed into the motion. Each push inside him was bliss and he was climbing so fast he knew he was close.

His own cock was trapped between them, and he didn't even need to touch himself as his orgasm chased down his spine. He came so hard he closed his eyes and lost himself to a deep kiss. Beneath him, around him, Zeph was coming with words of praise on his tongue.

The feelings subsided and gently Zeph lowered Nick to the bed again. Nothing was awkward, no pain, no real mess—Zeph took care of it all, then drew Nick close and spooned in from behind. Nick was warm and loved and covered in thin blankets. He felt like this was the nearest to perfection he would ever reach.

Zeph cleared his throat. "I researched something."

"What?"

Zeph's voice was quiet and respectful. "All the written records state that your father was a good man. The register says he loved your mom to the point where he went against the whole Klauson family to be with her. Did you know that?"

"Not really. All information about my dad is like a big family secret."

Zeph sighed. "He died not long after you were born, but he's always with you in spirit."

"I know nothing about him," Nick said sadly.

"His name was James, and he had the heart of an angel, strong and steadfast."

"My mom said she never knew who he was." Nick couldn't help the grief that wound inside him.

Zeph tightened his hold momentarily. "That was part of the deal, Nick. She *will* be able to tell you now. Part of the agreement for you staying with the family was that you would never be told. That was your great-grandfather's decision."

Nick turned in his arms. "How is it that you know all of this?"

Zeph kissed him gently. "Because I know angels. I spoke to one who was looking after your father and the day he died was a sad day for all angels."

"Do we all have an angel that tracks us?"

"Not everyone. Just those few with a purpose in life and a pure heart." He gently touched Nick's chest. "Like your heart."

"You know exactly what to say, don't you?" Nick observed.

Zeph chuckled and kissed Nick again. "I love you, and we are lucky to have met in such a way that I can allow myself to feel. Together we are strong."

"Strong enough to take down a necromancer?"

Zeph closed his eyes briefly, and his brow furrowed in a frown. "With the vampire, the wolf, and Sam—who is some of one thing and some of another?—yes, we can do it if we stick together."

Together they lay. Nick felt Zeph leave him at some ungodly hour of the morning, but he turned over and relaxed back toward sleep.

I'm falling in love with you, he thought.

"I know," came the soft reply from Zeph. *"We are going to win this and be together forever. Sleep now."*

Chapter Eleven

"SAMMMMM, WAKE UP, SAM."

Sam yanked the blanket over his head. Why would he want to wake up? In bed, he was warm and cozy and no one was trying to eat him, or kill him or declare he had powers he really didn't. Nope, not getting up.

"Go away," he mumbled. He didn't even open his eyes. He knew who was trying to get him to wake.

"But it's time to get up and visit Mal."

Sam pulled the blankets down. For that he'd get up. He looked into the amused eyes of his lover. "What?"

"For Mal, you'll get up, but for me, the comfy blankets win?"

"They'd win more if you were in here with me. What are you doing up so early anyway? Aren't you supposed to slumber during the day?"

Bob shook his head. "Why must you cling to your stereotypes? I was up talking to Hartman."

"I take it you two have an idea?"

"We're going back to the school to let Hart sniff around. He says necromancers always have an ashy smell, as does anyone who hangs around them for very long. He thinks he might be able to scent if anyone has been helping him in the school."

"Why don't you just ask Ariel?"

"She can't identify him. Some sort of barrier on her memory. I asked." Bob's smug smile had Sam pulling the blankets back over his head. It was too early to deal with lovers who knew everything.

"Go away."

"Mal."

Sam sighed. "Fine." Throwing back the blankets, he sat up in bed.

"Nice." Bob's eyes glowed with lust as he swept Sam with his gaze.

Sam laughed. "You've seen me naked before."

"Each time is just as good as the last. Wait, what's that?" Bob pointed to a spot on Sam's chest. A silvery circle glowed over the spot where Sam's heart lay beneath the skin.

Sam sighed. "Probably some more magic crap. Give me a minute to shower, and I'll join you and Hart downstairs."

Bob grabbed Sam's wrist. "Aren't you the least bit curious about the mark?"

"No. I'm becoming sort of numb to the entire magic thing. Nothing really surprises me anymore." Sam didn't know if it made him happy or jaded that there were few things left that shocked him.

Not too long ago, he'd been surprised to have a vampire for a lover. Now it was just one more thing he took for granted.

Bob yanked Sam closer until he could snag Sam around the waist and press their bodies together. "Never think I don't wake up every morning and adore the fact that you're mine."

Sam melted into Bob's kiss. The vampire gripped Sam's

hair in a firm fist, holding him immobile for Bob's attention. He hated to admit it, but Sam adored it when Bob went all alpha on him.

A sting to his bottom lip ratcheted up his desire when Bob began to suck at the bit of blood he'd undoubtedly caused with his bite. Bob groaned and forcibly separated their bodies. "Go get your shower before I forget we have people waiting for us."

He gave Sam a little shove away, then smacked him on the ass.

"Hey!" Sam protested.

Bob smirked. "Don't tell me you didn't like that. You know I can read your mind."

Sam stomped away from his lover, slamming the bathroom door behind him. He really hated the mind-reading aspect of their relationship, but the few times he'd been able to cut Bob out of his head had bothered the vampire a great deal. It wasn't worth the damage to their relationship to block Bob's mental pillaging.

"Thank you, love!" Bob shouted through the door.

Sam shook his head as he started the shower. At least he couldn't complain about boredom. Some days he wished he could, but not today.

ZEPH EXAMINED the people collected in Sam's small office. They were definitely an interesting group. "Ariel, I think you should stay here today. I know it will hurt not to be grounded with Sam, but you're too vulnerable to the necromancer. It will be interesting to see if his power wanes without you near him."

"I'll watch over her." Teddy, the resident ghost, floated

through the ceiling. "I can let Sam know if there's a problem."

"Thank you, Teddy," Sam said.

A new vibration in Sam's voice sent a trickle of power into the air, making Zeph shiver. Sam's eyes glowed silver for a moment.

What the celestial being is this?

"You're welcome, Sam." The ghost beamed with joy at Sam's thanks.

Bob put his hand on Sam's shoulder and the glow dimmed a little.

"What's the plan?" Zeph asked. He had some ideas of how things would work, but if Sam didn't agree, he doubted any of the others would go along with it.

"I want to go back to the school and let Hart sniff around. I also want to talk to Horace, the deputy head teacher. I'm worried he might be involved."

Zeph frowned. "Why do you think that?"

"Ariel has only said the necromancer was a man so the headmistress can't be the one responsible. We need to figure out what happened to her. I think he knows more than he's telling," Sam said.

Zeph nodded. "Sounds like a good place to start."

ZEPH FOLLOWED Nick up the steps to the school. A dangerous aura emitted from the building that hadn't been there when they left it last.

"I don't like this, Zeph," Nick whispered.

"The building can't hear you." Zeph couldn't resist teasing his man.

"I'm not so sure of that." Nick's gaze rested on the

gargoyles perched on the outside of the building. One was discernibly missing.

"It'll be all right." Zeph wrapped a hand around Nick's waist. "I won't let anything happen to you."

"He likes angel magic. You're more in danger than I am."

Zeph didn't want to admit Nick might have a point. "He took Ariel's powers because she wasn't expecting it. I'm not such an easy mark."

"Good." Nick slid his fingers through Zeph's, holding on to him as if he would protect him from harm.

Hart led the way of their small mixed paranormal troop. The shifter growled as he inhaled.

"Do you smell anything?" Sam asked.

"Zombies, bad magic, deception." Hartman spoke in short, choppy sentences, as if his wolf half had taken over and made it difficult for him to speak.

"Well, there were zombies here and definitely bad magic. It's the deception we're worried about," Sam replied.

Horace met them in the foyer.

"I didn't expect to see you back so quickly." Horace rushed forward with his hands extended in welcome.

"We have some more questions." Bob took the lead. Zeph watched in surprise as Sam stepped back and let him. He hadn't realized Bob and Sam had such an equal relationship.

"Of course," Horace said politely. "Please come with me to my office. I have coffee and wine and cookies, we can talk out of the range of little ears." He rubbed his hands together and a sly grin curved on his little gnome face.

Zeph's wings vibrated at a sudden press of magic somewhere in the school. Something was so very wrong here. He glanced around but didn't see any of the kids about—shouldn't they be running in the halls, or looking through the stair posts?

"Where are all your students?"

"Oh, they are off doing their studies. All in their rooms now," Horace said vaguely.

"Good. We'll stop and see Mal before we go," Bob said.

Horace stumbled but quickly caught and steadied himself. "Of course. That would be perfectly fine. After we have had our meeting, you will be free to see Mal."

Zeph narrowed his eyes as he watched Horace lead them down the hall. Alarm bells rang in his head. This felt too much like a setup. His wings ruffled irritably. He hadn't survived as long as he had by following along like a foolish child and ignoring his instincts.

"Where's the headmistress?" Zeph asked, stopping in his tracks. "Did she ever return? Did you call the authorities over her disappearance?" Nick looked over at him with realization on his face. Seemed like he had reached a similar conclusion that not everything was right with the acting head of the school.

Horace turned around and scowled at Zeph. "I said I would talk once we got to my office. I will answer all your questions there."

"No. We're not going to your office." Zeph suspected once they entered the gnome's office, they might not find the way back out. He'd seen gnome mazes before. Once you stepped into one, you were lost. He bet his halo this was a trap. "We can talk in the hall."

"But the children will hear," Horace whined. He clenched his hands into fists, and there was frustration leaking from behind his formerly groveling and smug expression.

"You said the children were studying away from here and safe," Bob said.

Zeph nodded. "We want answers now, Gnome."

He folded his arms and waited. The others stopped beside him. No one questioned why Zeph had stopped.

Hartman, who up to now had been quiet, stepped forward and sniffed the gnome, who batted him away. "I thought it was Zeph, but you smell like angel magic and ash." A low growl rolled up the back of his throat.

The gnome attempted to look innocent, and Zeph could see the emotions as they skimmed his face. Concern, anger, and a self-satisfied smirk. "Do I?" he said. He pulled himself to full height, which wasn't much. Then he crossed his arms over his chest. A faint glow appeared around him, and Zeph stepped back. The angel magic the gnome was using to form a protective barrier around him was strong. "Is this the time I tell you that I'm the one with the angel magic and that when I stole it, she was absolutely delicious to taste?"

Zeph couldn't think what to do. He couldn't get through the angel barrier. No one could. It was the best defense a gnome gone bad could have.

Then Nick punched Horace. Right through the barrier and connecting with Horace's smug face. The gnome fell down, screaming. Was this shrieking gnome really one of the stronger necromancers that Zeph had ever seen? And how the hell had Nick broken through the shield?

"Nick!" Zeph's mouth dropped open in shock. "How the hell did you...? How...?"

"I hate bullies." Nick shrugged at the surprised expressions around him. "Especially bullies who think some angel shield can stop a Klauson."

Nick waved his hands and red and white colored ropes appeared out of nowhere. They slithered across the floor with a soft shush of sound.

Horace shouted in fear as the ropes wrapped around his arms and legs until he looked like a round, pudgy candy cane.

"What are you doing?" There was very real fear in Horace's voice. Evidently, he thought having an angel shield was enough to protect him.

"Stopping you," Nick snapped.

"I run this school! You can't leave the children without supervision."

Zeph considered the gnome carefully. One minute, he was shouting that he was this great strong evil being, the next he was a sniveling mess on the floor and demanding to have his job back with children.

"You're not going back to that school," Zeph said firmly. He didn't like to mention that any being who dared to steal angel magic was not long for the mortal realm at all. Back home, there was a whole list of punishments that Horace could be given.

"Talking of the school, what did you do to the headmistress?" Nick asked.

Zeph huffed to himself. There was no way they were going to get anything from Horace. He wasn't going to implicate himself. Zeph couldn't believe it when instead of silence, or lies, Horace opened his mouth and words blurted out.

"I sent her south to a cabin I have near Sludge Monster Swamp." The gnome's eyes opened wide. "Why did I tell you that?"

Zeph stepped up to his lover. "Why did he tell you that?"

The blinding smile Nick turned on him warmed Zeph to his toes. "I might not have a lot of abilities, but Wonder Woman's lasso has nothing on my candy canes of truth. How do you think we know if kids are naughty or nice? You think they're going to tell us the truth if they've been awful all year?"

"Huh. You're just full of surprises."

Nick stopped smiling. "No, that's pretty much all I have now. Candy canes and truth."

Zeph cupped Nick's face between his palms. He hated it when Nick put himself down. "Hey, you did amazing. It would've taken us a lot longer to get him to tell us the truth. Now can you ask him some more? How long do these things last?"

"Only a few hours. Any more and it starts to affect their mind."

Sam stepped forward. "Where are the kids?" he demanded.

The gnome remained silent, and to Zeph's eyes, he looked smug.

"Sorry, Sam, it only works if I ask the questions," Nick said.

Sam nodded. "Oh, all right. Could you ask him what he did with the children please?"

Nick repeated the question.

The gnome rolled his eyes. "They are in the south wing. I locked them in there. They kept getting into my potions and messing with my curses, and people think I'm evil! They never had to deal with a school full of little delinquents."

He sounded so put upon Zeph had to bite his lip to stop from laughing.

Then Nick asked the one thing Zeph didn't want to hear an answer to. Ever since he'd seen Ariel in ghost form, he'd known the answer. He just didn't want to believe Ariel was dead.

"What did you do to Ariel?"

Horace narrowed his eyes. "I stripped that bitch of her magic. It's not like she was using it. But she got even in the end. She turned out to be my soul mate. I killed her and lost half of myself. I can't sleep. I can barely eat. I'm a fraction of the gnome I was before."

Horace made a weird face like he was attempting to suck the words back into his mouth. Zeph couldn't help wondering how Ariel fell for the nasty creature in the first place, but Ariel had always had strange taste.

"Ask him if he bewitched her into falling for him," Zeph asked.

Nick nodded. "Did you bewitch Ariel into falling for your lies?"

"Yes. It was easy. When she looked at me, she saw a handsome prince."

Zeph felt sadness curl inside him. Poor Ariel was only ever looking for her one true Prince. That it turned out to be a vicious lying gnome was just the worst thing.

Nick continued. "How can we give her magic back to her?"

Horace shrugged as far as the ropes let him. "If I knew that, I could get her off my back. There's nothing romantic about a ghost following you around. I don't care what the storybooks say."

Zeph stepped in. "There's nothing further he can do for us. I'm going to take him to the angel council for sentencing."

"What! Wait!" Horace shouted. "I didn't do anything wrong."

"What do you mean you didn't do anything wrong?" Sam shouted at the gnome. "You are responsible for the dragon king dying. You brainwashed a dragon shifter, resurrected zombies at the bottom of a school, stripped an angel of her powers then killed her. You're evil."

"And you're not exactly a proper role model for children," Bob pointed out.

"Exactly," Sam agreed.

"I'm a necromancer. I can't help it if I behave according to my nature," the gnome brushed off Sam's accusations.

Zeph grabbed the gnome off the floor and dumped him over one shoulder. He kissed Nick on the forehead before stepping away from the group. "I'm going to take him with me. I'll be back in a bit."

The last he said while staring at Nick. He didn't want the elf to think he was running off on him.

Nick smiled. "See you."

"Yes, you will," Zeph agreed.

Closing his eyes, he focused on home.

Chapter Twelve

ZEPH KNEW SOMETHING WAS WRONG AS SOON AS HE SET FOOT in his home. Two of his more vocal brothers sat waiting for him, and both looked like the smug idiots that they were.

"Sim, Gad, what can I do for you?"

Both angels stood and observed him silently. There had to be a reason for Simiel, general badass internal affairs angel, and Gadreel, angel of all things warfare, to have shown up but instead of speaking they stared.

"What?" Zeph's patience snapped.

"What is that?" Sim asked. He pointed at Zeph, and for a moment, Zeph didn't get the question. Then he realized what Sim was pointing at, and with a heave of his shoulder, he unceremoniously dropped Horace to the ground. When the gnome hit the stones, some of the candy ropes cracked but not enough for Horace to escape.

"Business," Zeph explained evenly. Each angel had their roles and the non-interference rule kept other angels from butting in on each other's jobs. Be it destroying cities or rescuing Santa's nephew, Zeph's business was private.

Gad leaned over the semi-conscious gnome, then backed

away in horror. "He has Ariel's magic," he whispered. "What happened?"

"Nothing you need to worry about," Zeph pointed out. "Now I have things to do, so if you'll excuse me?" He waved a hand to the door of the landing station, motioning his brothers to leave.

"You've been called," Gad said. Sim nodded next to him. Was it just Zeph, or did Gad and Sim both look pleased? Gad had never entirely gotten over Zeph beating him to the Angel of Vengeance gig and Sim was a follower.

"What for this time?" he asked, even though he knew in his heart exactly why he had been called. Someone had clearly found out about Nick.

"Midnight in the Gold Court, Zephariel, Angel of Vengeance," Gad stated.

Zeph's heart sunk. He'd been in emerald, and twice in silver, but never had anything he'd done warranted the High Court. Then he was buoyed by the recollection that most of the Gold Court owed him favors. He'd be fine. Nick would be fine. They couldn't actually touch Nick anyway, being as the angels had a long held peace pact with most branches of the supernatural tree. Add to that Nick was half human and angels couldn't hurt humans however much they might want to.

Gad walked out of the room, and Sim shrugged. "Whatever you did, little brother, I hope it was worth it."

Zeph nodded. "It was worth it."

Trying to kill time while he waited for his appointment, Zeph took Horace to be processed for his crimes. Justice was swift. The administrator of the Justice Department stripped the gnome of every molecule of celestial magic, and in a few minutes, he was just a sniveling small thing who begged for his mommy.

"What do you want me to do with him?" Hamaliel looked up from the book of time and stared pointedly at Zeph. Always the one who crossed the Ts and dotted the Is, Hamaliel was OCD about filling out the right forms.

"I guess we could send him back." They didn't have prisons there, and no one actually ever got sent *downstairs* to the hot place. Not if there was any way the criminals' souls could be re-used. "Can we do that?" Zeph asked. Not that he wanted leniency for the little creature. After all, he'd threatened Nick, but he wouldn't ever willingly send anyone to the next world if they could be remade.

Hamaliel clicked his fingers. "Done." Horace the Gnome vanished, leaving nothing in his wake.

"What did you send him back as?"

"A baby bird on a cliff," Hamaliel said dismissively.

Zeph would have preferred slug, but he'd take the baby bird instead. "What about Ariel?"

Hamaliel ran a finger down names in the book. "She's on my list to return to the pool." Then he peered around Zeph. "Next," he called. Turning the page in the book, he licked the end of his pencil and again stared up at Zeph. "You can go," he said.

Zeph realized he was standing like he was stuck in mud, and with a start, he left the Hall of Records.

Midnight was getting closer, only a few minutes away, and he made the decision to get to the Court in advance of everyone else. If he could manage to talk to any of the five angels that sat in the Gold Court, then maybe he could call in some favors. After striding down the wide hallways, he pushed opened the door of the Court and entered into chaos.

Scarlet and green covered everything and angels had a cage of light around someone kneeling in the middle of the Court. With growing horror, Zeph realized he'd been given the wrong time. Somehow this Court was very much in progress. Not only that but Nick was here, naked and kneeling, wrapped in chains in front of the masses of viewers. Evidenced by the candy stripes everywhere, Nick had obviously struggled with his captors.

Zeph could see Gad and Sim looking directly at him.

"*Sorry*," Gad mouthed. He didn't look very sorry—in fact, he looked smug.

Zeph strode farther into the room and stood directly in front of Nick. He couldn't look inside the cage—he couldn't show any weakness, and if he saw Nick in any pain, he would lose his control there and then.

"Zeph," Nick's voice was anguished, and Zeph's heart broke a little.

"With respect, I was told the Court convened at midnight," he said to the five judges who sat on high, and to an angel, they frowned down at him.

Raziel, the leader of the court, banged a gavel to stop the level of chatter in the forum space. "Zephariel, Angel of Vengeance, you will take your place on the stand."

Zeph knew better than to argue, or to beg for Nick to be released. Resolutely, he stalked to the stand and climbed the steps that put him almost level with the five judges. He was friends with three of them, knew a fourth through a mishap involving a Roman soldier. Raziel was the unknown here.

"Zephariel, you are brought here to this place to account for the crime of taking a human lover. How do you answer this assertion?"

"He is my fated mate," Zeph said clearly. A collective gasp went through the throng of angels around the room. Clearly Zeph being on trial was enough to warrant one hell of an audience.

"Angels do not have fated mates. Scratch that from the

book," Raziel demanded. The scribe took his quill and drew a line through the statement that had magically appeared on the paper. A single burst of flame and it was gone. "Now begin again."

Zeph was utterly determined that the words confirming he and Nick were fated mates would remain in the book for perpetuity. "Nicholas Klauson is my fated mate," he said clearly. Again the noise in the auditorium grew. The words appeared in the book, and the scribe looked up at Raziel for guidance.

"Scratch the words," he ordered. The scribe immediately did what he was told. "Zephariel, I give you one last chance to tell me the absolute truth before I cast this human back to earth and lock you down for a millennium."

Zeph's breath caught in his chest. To be apart from Nick just these short hours was suffering enough, but to be released from incarceration, knowing his lover was long since dead, would kill him as sure as any arrow. If the words were enough to have this happen, then actions needed to show more. Very carefully, he stepped down from the stand.

Raziel peered over the judges' bench and his thick eyebrows drew together in consternation. "What are you doing?" he asked with disbelief in his voice.

"I choose to be mortal."

The words immediately appeared in the book and the room was deadly silent. The horror of what Zeph had chosen to do was not something an angel gasped at. It was the end of things. A mortal life was so short.

"No!" Nick shouted from the cage. "I won't let you."

Zeph extended his wings to their full extent, aware that as one of the warrior angels, he was impressive and dominated the room.

"Nick may be half human, but he is wholly mine. I wish

to be mortal and to return to the home of Sam Enderson with Nick." He knew he had to be specific, otherwise the Angels would likely take Nick and place him in Siberia, with Zeph lost in the middle of a wide ocean.

"You realize the implications of what you are saying? This man-elf is your undoing if you throw everything away for…" Raziel stopped. He clearly didn't have the words. Over the centuries, a few angels had chosen this path—just a few… of thousands.

"For love," Zeph answered simply. He tucked his wings back in and bowed his head.

"You can't, Zeph—think about what you're doing!" Nick shouted. The words spun in Zeph's head. He knelt on the floor at the other side of the cage bars and looked in at Nick. He'd clearly fought being there. If the red and green stripes weren't enough indication, then surely the bruises and cuts on his body were.

"You're hurt," Zeph said softly. "I am so sorry."

A single tear rolled down Nick's face. "It's not your fault we fell in love. I wish I were better for you, a full elf, not with human blood. Then it wouldn't matter."

Zeph's heart ripped open. Nick thought he wasn't good enough? That he wished he was better for Zeph? That wasn't right.

"You make me whole," Zeph said firmly. Around him voices rose in astonishment at something in the court, but Zeph didn't move. If they sent Nick away and tried to imprison him, then he would fight with every breath he had to make his way to Nick's side.

"I love you, Zeph!" Nick shouted over the noise. "I always will."

"You need to stand up, Zephariel," a soft, feminine voice said. Zeph looked up and into the beautiful ethereal face of

Ariel. She remained in ghost form. She smiled at him as he clambered to stand.

"You're home," he said to her.

"Thanks to you and your companions. Thank you, Zeph. I wish I could help you now."

Zeph bowed his head a little, then watched in amazement as she touched the golden cage and her hand went straight through it. With a small movement, she created a space into which Zeph could climb, and within seconds, Zeph was inside and holding Nick close.

"Are you okay?" he asked a little desperately. Nick was in a bad way, his face covered in blood, his neck marked with gashes. Temper rose in Zeph that Nick had been treated so badly.

"'M'fine," Nick mumbled. Zeph didn't call him on the lie, just held him firm and close.

"Ariel, you will leave the chamber," Raziel ordered loudly.

Ariel looked at Nick and smirked a little. She always was a firebrand, hence her job as supernatural liaison—the same job that had inevitably put her in the way of the gnome and his damn desires for power.

"Shut up, you windbag," she called up to Raziel.

"Ariel—"

"I've know you for millennia, Raziel, and you'll never change. Remember the times you've fallen in love and tell me these two are not in love. Fated mates or not, you cannot deny them happiness."

"Your words mean nothing here, ghost," Raziel added the last word with a hint of derision. The crowd hissed disapproval, and Raziel seemed to realize what he'd done. Ariel was popular. When she'd disappeared, a lot of people had tried to track her, rewards had been offered, angels of all walks had wanted to help. Raziel, on the other hand, was the big, bad guy with the power that he seemed to enjoy throwing about far too much.

"I think you're the odd one out here," Ariel said. She floated toward the judges' bench and hovered right in Raziel's face. "Do you wish me to tell them all I have seen?" she asked innocently. Raziel went bright red.

"Enough," he said and smacked the gavel on the desk. "Mortality is granted."

"No," Ariel said firmly.

"What do you mean no? It's what he wanted."

"What he wants is to be with the one he loves, his fated mate. If you separate them, then Zephariel will lose his mind. You will allow him to remain as he is, and you will let the two of them leave."

"That is unheard of," Raziel blustered.

Nick moved in Zeph's arm, struggling to stand. "What is she doing?" he asked. Zeph helped his lover to his feet, and together, they stood to face whatever was thrown at them.

"She's helping us," Zeph said with conviction. There was no way he was going to let Nick see or feel the panic inside him.

"Your last chance, Raziel," Ariel said firmly. As one, the room began to chatter.

"Enough!" Raziel banged his gavel. The room fell silent. "This is making a mockery of celestial law."

Ariel tilted her ghostly head a little in consideration. "That happened in Atlantis as well, or so I heard," she said loud enough for everyone to hear.

This time Raziel paled. Then he banged the gavel twice. "The human will be returned to Sam Enderson. Zephariel is free to go." He vanished. As did the court, the other angels around them, and the cage surrounding Zeph and Nick. Only Ariel remained.

"Thank you," Zeph said simply.

"Don't thank me," Ariel replied. "Take your man home and live a long life, Zephariel." Then she vanished.

Zeph moved his attention to Nick. Tenderly, he tilted Nick's head back and winced at the blood. He attempted to heal the wounds, but nothing worked. Evidently, this all needed to heal on its own.

"Close your eyes, Nick," he ordered gently. Nick didn't argue. Exhaling noisily, he closed his eyes and slumped against Zeph. In the blink of an eye, they were back in the safety of Sam's house, in the office with the smoky walls. After gathering Nick up in his arms, he stalked up to the room they had been sharing and laid him lovingly on the bed.

"What happened?" Bob asked urgently from the door. "One minute he was here, the next he vanished."

Zeph didn't even have the words to explain what had happened. "I need medicine for Nick. He's hurt badly."

Bob crossed to the bed to examine Nick. "I'll get it." He left the room to fetch whatever he thought he needed. When he returned, a few minutes later, Sam was with him. Between the three of them they cleaned the worst of Nick's wounds. Zeph half hoped that Sam's touch would heal Nick, but it didn't. When Nick finally slept, Bob and Sam left the room and shut the door behind them. Nick hadn't woken up in all the time he was being cleaned and his wounds dealt with. Zeph refused to show it, but he'd seen angelic wounds before and he was desperate with worry.

Finally, Nick was dressed in a pair of sweat pants and a soft worn tee that Sam had said was his. Zeph gathered his unconscious love and held him close.

"I love you, Nick. Come back to me."

Chapter Thirteen

NICK COULD HEAR A VOICE CALLING TO HIM. HE DIDN'T understand the words, but the coaxing tone piqued his interest. Who was talking to him? He hurt. His body ached and burned from what surely must be a million tiny cuts.

"That's it, love, open your eyes."

Zeph!

Nick's eyelids flicked open. His angel lay beside him. Zeph's wings spread around them both like a feather blanket.

"I hurt, Zeph."

"I know, love. I'm sorry. Can you tell me who did it? I'll make sure they suffer for what they've done."

Nick shook his head. He sucked in a breath when that motion caused waves of pain to roll through his body.

Zeph huffed his disapproval at the effort. "Don't move. You're pretty banged up. Nothing permanent, but no one seems to be able to heal you. Even Sam's freaky powers didn't kick in."

"Are you here to stay?"

Zeph frowned. "Didn't you hear what I said? No one can heal you. I don't know what to do, but someone is going to pay. I'm going to go back to heaven and kick my brothers' asses."

"No." Nick wrapped a hand around Zeph's arm. "I need you here. Who knows if they will keep you if you step a wing in heaven right now. That judge had a twitch about harming you. They are aching for any reason to strip you of your wings. I can't let that happen."

"I am a warrior angel, the Angel of Vengeance. I can't let them get away with harming you." Zeph's hard expression didn't soften.

Nick pushed through the pain in his head. "Stay with me and show them that you made the right decision. The best way to prove them wrong is to live a long and happy life with me. They aren't worth the heartache of fighting."

Zeph pressed a soft kiss to Nick's cheek. "Fighting for you is always worth it."

If he didn't already love the angel, Nick knew he would've fallen right then. "I want you to stay here. For me."

Zeph's wings vibrated slightly from the tension in his shoulders. He'd closed his eyes as if the sight of Nick's injuries were too much for him.

"Hey, look at me. I'm not going to lose you over this. I need you to be strong enough to not go after the angels who roughed me up. You don't have to promise to be best friends with them, but I won't have a vendetta on my conscience."

Zeph opened his eyes. The love in his expression made Nick's breath catch in his chest.

"If that is what it takes to make you happy. I will abide by your request, but I will no longer acknowledge them as my kin." The statement was final, and Nick realized there would be no more discussion.

Nick hoped Zeph would mend his relationships over time, but with his body aching and pain radiating across his skin, he didn't have the willpower to insist Zeph hug it out. If Zeph wanted to dislike the angels who beat Nick up, then at the moment, he was more than okay with that.

"Thank you."

Zeph kissed Nick's forehead again. "You're welcome."

"There are other parts of me you can kiss," Nick offered.

His lover's smile lacked its usual glow. "You are badly injured. I don't want to hurt you."

Nick closed his eyes again. "I'm going to go back to sleep for a bit." He'd used up all his energy talking.

"You do that. I'll be here."

The conviction in Zeph's voice that he'd rather lay beside Nick than do anything else in the world soothed Nick back to sleep.

A SCREAM WOKE NICK UP. He bolted upright only to give a shout of his own when his body protested the movement.

"Hey, easy." Zeph rubbed a large warm hand along Nick's back, careful of Nick's injuries.

Nick melted in his touch. "Who screamed?"

"I don't know."

"Want to go check?" No way could Nick rest easy if someone was in trouble. He couldn't sense any danger, but that didn't mean none existed.

"I don't want to leave you alone."

"I'll be fine."

Zeph paused but eventually nodded and slid out of bed. Nick admired the muscular lines of his mate's body. If he had even one less injury, he would've jumped the angel.

Soft laughter had him dragging his gaze to Zeph's face. "What?"

"I can practically feel your gaze on me."

"Is that a bad thing?"

Zeph groaned. "Not when you're healthy enough for me to screw you against the wall. When you're injured, then yes, it can be a bad thing for my poor cock." He gazed mournfully down at his erection.

Nick chuckled. "Get dressed and find out about our screamer."

Grinning, Zeph slipped on a pair of soft gray sweats. He left his chest bare, not bothering to dress to cover his wings. Nick figured that made sense. It wasn't like anyone in Sam's house should be unaware of Zeph's presence.

ZEPH CURSED under his breath as he left his mate alone in the bedroom they shared. He'd have to find them a permanent place. His place in heaven wouldn't do anymore. Did Nick have a house at the North Pole? Was that where Santas lived, or did they only tell people that so they wouldn't be bothered?

He met Sam on the landing, with Bob not far behind. "Hey, Zeph, you heard the scream too?"

"Yeah, I was hoping you knew what it was."

"No clue," Sam said. "We were going to investigate."

"I'll come with," Zeph said. He didn't want anything to happen to his hosts. He also didn't want whatever screamed to come close to his mate.

Bob opened his mouth as if to protest, but an elbow to the stomach from Sam had him closing it again.

The trio headed down the stairs. Teddy floated through the ceiling to the lower level. For a ghost, he appeared concerned. "I think it came from outside."

Sam walked ahead of the group. Without waiting for his

lover to catch up, he yanked the door open. A woman stood on the other side. Her clothes were in disarray, her hat drunkenly tilted on her head, and her eyes were so wide it was surprising to Zeph that anything else had room on her face.

"Ms. Triplewine? What are you doing here?" Sam asked.

"Mr. Enderson? Are you…? Do you… live here?" Her gaze was unfocused as if her mind wasn't quite up to the task of conversation.

Sam nodded. "Would you like to come in? We've all been wondering where you went."

"Y-yes, I would." Her hands shook as she walked past them into the foyer.

"Have you been back to the school yet?" Bob asked.

Zeph wondered how the kids were doing. He knew they were left in the hands of the teachers, but with so much going on, they could be stressed.

Ms. Triplewine shook her head. "I don't know where I am."

Zeph frowned. "May I touch your head?"

She nodded. The confused expression on her face didn't change. Zeph pressed his fingers to her temples. A bright light flared between his hands. He let her go.

"What did you do?" Bob asked.

"She had a spell placed on her. I'm surprised she made it here." Zeph shook his hands, trying to remove the tendrils of sensation tingling through them.

"Oh, thank you," Ms. Triplewine's eyes were clearer and she crackled with energy. "I feel so much better. I don't suppose I can persuade one of you gentlemen to give me a ride back to the school. I have no idea how I got here."

"Did you scream?" Bob asked.

The headmistress scowled at Bob. "What do you mean, did I scream?"

"We heard someone screaming." Zeph offered.

Ms. Triplewine shook her head. "Not that I remember. But I was confused."

"I screamed."

Zeph looked down at the tiny gargoyle he'd rescued from the school. "Why?"

The gargoyle fluttered its wings and landed on a table in the entryway with a loud thud. "Because I saw a cat running around. I'm afraid of cats."

Sam rubbed his temples and looked stressed. Zeph didn't blame him.

"Did you want to be returned to the school?" Zeph asked.

"No. I'm a familiar. I want to find my person. I've been watching that damned building for three hundred years, and he hasn't shown up yet. It's about time I went to look for him."

Ms. Triplewine pursed her lips together in a tight bow like a school librarian Zeph had once gotten into an altercation with.

"So you are just going to abandon your duties and run off?" she asked, her tone disapproving.

"Yep." The gargoyle fluttered his wings. If he were a bird, Zeph would've thought he was fluffing them.

The headmistress rolled her eyes. "Fine, but don't come flying back to me when you want another job."

"Somehow I think I can find another building to perch on." The gargoyle's dry tone had Zeph biting his lips to hold back his laughter. This conversation was surreal.

"Why don't we go back to the school?" Bob said diplomatically. He escorted the headmistress outside with Sam trailing after.

"They are a strange couple," the gargoyle commented.

"I'm going to go check on Nick." If Zeph stood in the foyer for even one more second, he would burst out laughing. He'd had the strangest day so far. Good thing he had Nick upstairs. He loved the fact he had someone to tell funny stories to.

He ran up the stairs and opened the door. He came to a screeching halt when he realized that Nick no longer was alone in the room. Beside him stood a man with a snowy white beard, a rosy red nose, and a belly so large he could barely reach down to touch Nick.

Wait…

"What are you doing?"

"Well, hello there!" That large man turned to look at Zeph and grinned broadly. "I'm Nicholas's uncle, Santa Klauson."

"Yeah, I kind of figured that, but what are you doing?" Zeph twitched to rain down some angel fire on the man touching his Nick. He didn't like it when other people had contact with his mate. They never treated him properly.

"I'm healing Nicholas from the damage you allowed others to do to him." Santa's grin faded as he explained, and his eyebrows joined together when he scowled, forming a furry white caterpillar. It distracted Zeph for a moment from his words.

"I didn't let Nick be injured. It was out of my control." And didn't it hurt to admit that?

"It wasn't his fault," Nick defended Zeph.

"Of course not, dear boy. You are always the quickest to defend people. Now stay still so I can heal you with Christmas magic."

Zeph wanted to rail against the white-haired elf elder, but he'd rather Nick be healed than for him to get his two cents in.

A tinkling noise like a dozen chimes rang through the room and small white sparkles lit the air. Even after seeing a great many feats of magic in heaven and on earth, Zeph had to privately admit Santa magic was in a category of spectacular all by itself. He didn't dare speak; he barely breathed as a crisp winter wind slid through the room. Zeph thought he tasted a bit of snow.

"Be healthy, Nicholas. You might only be half an elf, but you have the heart of a giant," Santa said.

Before Zeph could agree with that statement, Santa pinned him with a look. "I'm going to be back here at Christmas. Remember to tell Mal that the kids who get the best presents are the ones who put out eggnog and sugar cookies, heavy on the sprinkles. None of that low-fat or gluten-free crap either."

"I'll remember," Zeph promised.

Santa looked back at Nick. "Take care, Nick. I'll see you soon. It's almost time for another Klauson get-together. I don't think anyone will pick on you with your new partner."

"You knew about people bullying him and didn't do anything?" Zeph asked.

"I'm sorry to say I didn't know everything that was going on. I still don't. But Nicholas is an important member of my team, and if you catch anyone telling him otherwise, you have my permission to take care of them." Santa's expression was far from jolly.

"Thank you, I will."

"Good. I left you a present." Santa winked at Zeph, then disappeared.

"Whoa, I didn't know he actually did that."

Nick nodded. "Yeah, the whole up-the-chimney thing is bull. He can go in and out of anywhere with his Christmas magic."

"What did he mean about leaving us a present?"

Nick scanned the room. "I think he means that." He pointed a small bottle with a ribbon around its neck.

Zeph snatched it off the table. "Candy cane flavored lube. There's something seriously wrong about getting that from Santa." Zeph said, horrified.

Nick laughed. "He's not a father of twenty for nothing."

"Twenty? Seriously?"

Nick nodded. "He was ecstatic when I told him I was gay and didn't plan to add to the family."

"You don't want kids?"

Nick wrinkled his nose. "Not really. Is that a deal breaker?"

"Nope." Relief swept through Zeph. "I don't want any either."

"Good. I feel much better now. Why don't we get in the Christmas spirit?"

Zeph laughed. "I think I can agree to that."

Epilogue

SAM, BOB, AND MAL RETURNED. MAL RUSHED UP TO HER room while Bob and Sam went to his office. "I'm glad we settled the necromancer matter," Sam said, sitting behind his desk.

"Me too." Bob perched on the corner of Sam's desk. "Whatever will we do with all our free time?"

Bob's eyes gleamed with lust.

Sam smiled. "I'm sure we can think of something."

Bob leaned in for a kiss.

"Excuse me."

Bob groaned over the interruption.

Laughing, Sam turned his head to watch the new gargoyle hopping into the room.

"Can I help you?"

"That creepy cat said you could help me find my master."

"I can try." Sam couldn't deny the gargoyle, not if Smudge said he could help. They had an agreement, after all.

"Good. I help you. You help me."

"What do you think you can help me with?" Sam hoped he hadn't just gained a second gargoyle for his house. The small creature looked around the room thoughtfully, then pointed triumphantly at the gargoyle on Sam's desk.

"I can tell you that that isn't a real gargoyle," he said.

"If he's not a gargoyle, what is he?" Bob asked.

The gargoyle shrugged, not an easy feat with stone wings. "I'm not sure, but he doesn't feel like a gargoyle. He is other."

"What do you mean by other?" Sam asked impatiently. He wished people, paranormals, whatever, would actually speak in a real language, not some mystical mumbo jumbo.

"Not of stone," the gargoyle explained patiently. Then he hopped closer and poked a stony finger at the other creature. "Other," he added dramatically.

"Crap." Sam didn't like it when words like *other* began to be tossed around. It never meant anything good.

"That isn't good," Bob pointed out. He leaned in and looked closer, and Sam swore the stone creature moved to turn his head. Not before Sam saw the little gargoyle's expression. How was it he had never noticed that his uncle's gargoyle had such a sad look carved into his face?

No. Bob was right.

Other was never a good thing.

THE END

The Case of the Purple Pearl
The Case of the Guilty Ghost

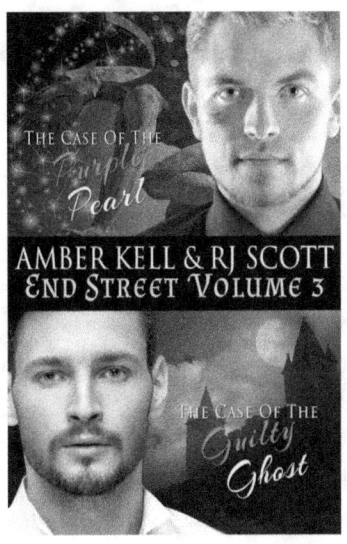

The Case of the Purple Pearl

After failing in a quest to win the Fae Queen's approval, Halstein is locked in a world of stone. Forced to remain a gargoyle he spends his days on Sam's desk pining for his lost love.

Prince Idris's lover went missing and was presumed dead. Alone, Idris lives a life away from court, starved of energy but unwilling to sleep in the room he once shared with his beloved.

Can Sam and Bob save these fated lovers before it's too

late? And will Bob's ultimate sacrifice be enough to free Hal from his prison?

The Case of the Guilty Ghost

Bob is lost in grief, Sam is fighting for his life, and there is no middle ground. Can their love survive?

Bob is grieving over his brother's sacrifice. Guilt-ridden and devastated, he buries himself in vampire mourning and pulls away from Sam.

Magic tears Sam from the vampire castle and he has to face new adversaries alone when all he wants is Bob at his side.

Ettore is in the Aset Ka waiting room, next in line for the ceremony for his soul to be torn from his body. Aset Ka has other plans, and Ettore finds himself reunited with a lost love and fighting alongside his brother.

A forgotten past binds Theodore 'Teddy' McCurray Constantine III to Ettore, and with the curse tied to Ettore broken by his death, Teddy's past returns to him with a vengeance.

A royal family in denial, a battle between gods, and long forgotten love leaves no time for Sam and Bob to take a breath. Is it too late to save the supernatural world?

Amber Kell

Amber Kell has made a career out of daydreaming. It has been a lifelong habit she practices diligently as shown by her complete lack of focus on anything not related to her fantasy world building.

When she told her husband what she wanted to do with her life, he told her to go have fun.

During those seconds she isn't writing, she remembers she has children who humor her with games of 'what if' and let her drag them to foreign lands to gather inspiration. Her youngest confided in her that he wants to write because he longs for a website and an author name—two things apparently necessary to be a proper writer.

Despite her husband's insistence she doesn't drink enough to be a true literary genius, she continues to spin stories of people falling happily in love and staying that way.

She is thwarted during the day by a traffic jam of cats on the stairway and a puppy who insists on walks, but she bravely perseveres.

amberkell.wordpress.com
amberkellwrites@gmail.com

Meet RJ Scott

RJ discovered romance in books at a very young age and realized that if there wasn't romance on the page, she could create it in her head. With over one hundred and fifty books published, she is a full time author of gay romance.

She lives and works out of her home in the beautiful English countryside, spends her spare time reading, watching films, and enjoying time with her family.

The last time she had a week's break from writing she didn't like it one little bit and has yet to meet a box of chocolates she couldn't defeat.

www.rjscott.co.uk | rj@rjscott.co.uk

NEWSLETTER - rjscott.co.uk/rjnews

instagram.com/rjscott_author

amazon.com/author/rj-scott

bookbub.com/authors/rj-scott

goodreads.com/rjscott

patreon.com/RJScott